HEROINES
OF THE KITCHEN TABLE

Stories of Survivors

Carol Lynn Luck

For Thea ~ a new friend & kindred spirit ~ May all our stories live on ~ With love Carol

Dedication

This novel is dedicated to all the courageous men and women past and present who fight for survival and equality in worlds where greed and power drive leaders to dehumanize others.

This novel is inspired by brave women I have known who survived the atrocities perpetrated by one man, Hitler, whose hunger for power knew no bounds. The propaganda that spread more rapidly than any plague turned people into blind followers who believed that all human beings are not created equal. The insanity that gripped Europe made inhumanity and injustice the norm. The police marched to the orders of their superiors, some demonstrated their savagery for advancement and ego, others followed orders just to survive themselves. It was a time of fear, atrocities and unimaginable horrors. Yet, the spirits of the ones who tell their stories live on.

CONTENTS

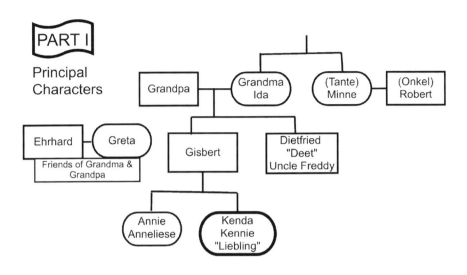

PART I

Principal Characters

- Grandpa — Grandma Ida
- (Tante) Minne — (Onkel) Robert
- Ehrhard — Greta — Friends of Grandma & Grandpa
- Gisbert
- Dietfried "Deet" Uncle Freddy
- Annie Anneliese
- Kenda Kennie "Liebling"

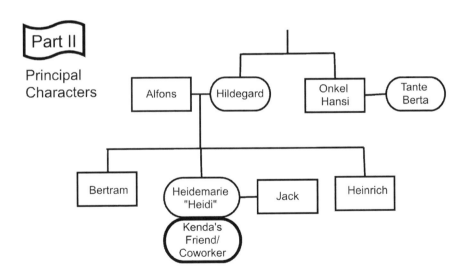

Part II

Principal Characters

- Alfons — Hildegard
- Onkel Hansi — Tante Berta
- Bertram
- Heidemarie "Heidi" — Jack — Kenda's Friend/Coworker
- Heinrich

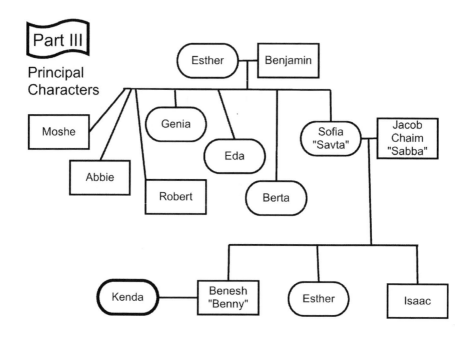

Part III

Principal
Characters

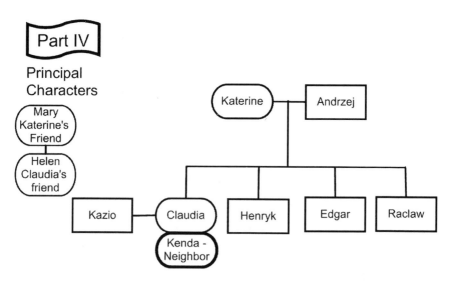

Part IV

Principal
Characters

Part V

Principal
Characters

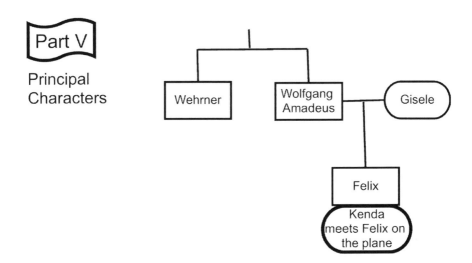

LOCATIONS

Some of the places in this novel belonged to different countries then and now.

After World War II, Germany surrendered, giving back to Poland: Neumark, most of Pomerania, and Silesia. These towns in Silesia became part of Poland and the names changed accordingly:

Neurode (Germany), now Nowa Ruda, Poland
Langenbielau (Germany), now Bielawa, Poland
Reichenbach (Germany), now Dzierzoniow, Poland

These three towns are less than 20 miles apart; by actual coincidence, they are important locations in both Grandma's and Savta's stories.

Sniatyn was part of Poland, now it is in the Ukraine. Karachi belonged to India, now it is in Pakistan.

Also note that Persia is now Iran; Palestine, Israel.

PART I

HUNGRY FOR POWER

Chapter One

Oklahoma City 1956

"It's so hot outside, over 100 degrees," Grandma said. I leaned my arms from my elbows to my wrists on her shiny white kitchen table. Grandpa told us that it's porcelain, which is cold even when the room is hot. Grandma's big body shuffled around the room, filling her salt and pepper shakers, washing the lunch dishes, and talking to me.

"Liebling, it's so wonderful to have you and your sister here for the summer. I wish you lived close enough that we could see each other every day instead of having you three days and three nights away. We moved here to keep the family together. Then your father got that job in Washington, D.C.," Grandma told me.

She talked funny so I had to listen carefully to know what she was saying. She made 'we' and 'will' sound like 've' and 'vill'. 'This' was 'dis'. 'D', 't' and 'th' in her words all sounded the same; 'Beth', 'bed' and 'bet' were 'bet' according to Grandma.

"Grandma, why do you talk in such strange English?"

"Well, you know we came here from Germany. Grandpa and I spoke German and Polish before we learned English."

"So what were you doing in Germany?" I asked.

"I was born there in Langenbielau, but that city belongs to Poland now." Grandma explained.

"Why did you come to America? If you didn't come here, would we have been born in Germany too?"

"It's a long story, Liebling."

"I like long stories, Grandma. Tell me."

Chapter Two

Langenbielau, Germany 1930

Grandma begins her story...

It all started one day when my good friend, Greta and I were going to town for food. We had little money, but we all helped each other. Life was hard. Many people had no work. Greta's husband, Erhard, and Grandpa were both carpenters, and people had no money to pay them to make anything. But we got by. The small yard was a garden of beets, onions, radishes and potatoes with a border of gooseberries and a big linden tree. We made tea from the dried linden flowers.

#

There was a lot of noise in the town square. A man stood up on a platform surrounded by a crowd of people. He was shouting, and everyone was listening. Greta and I stood among them near the platform. He was pleasant enough and very convincing. He talked about the Vaterland, Germany, rising to power again after the defeat of the war. He said our country was truly superior, and he promised to lead us to prosperity again. Everyone would have jobs and money for food, clothes, and nice homes. The crowd cheered and clapped as he spoke.

I didn't know about this man, what he said was too good to be true. Someone would have to pay. He stood too tall and straight, with his little mustache, and the look in his eyes was captivating and frightening! Standing there gave me chills and I pushed to go, but Greta whispered that we needed to hear him to the end. When his speech was finally over, we went on our way. My mind would not rest. We went straight to Greta's house. Grandpa was there with Erhard playing checkers and drinking schnapps. They wanted to know why we were gone for so long. Greta told our husbands about the man speaking in town. They agreed that maybe our country was due for better times.

I pounded my fist on the table and said, "Oh no! That man is hungry for power. It is clear to me that he will stop at nothing," I said with rage.

My ranting and raving continued until they all agreed. We made a plan to get out of Europe as soon as we could. Greta had a sister living in America, so she and Erhard would be able to go to her, with few questions asked by the authorities. If Grandpa went with them, he could find a job, send us money and then I'd be able to follow with the boys, Gisbert and Dietfried. With their father in America, we should be able to get passage to see him. That was the plan.

The very next day they went to the town hall and filed papers to get permission to leave the country. Then, there was nothing to do but wait. A month went by, then two, then three. We gave up, thinking the officials wouldn't let them go. But we dared not ask questions. Then papers came for Grandpa and the Reismans. They prepared quickly and then Greta, Ehrhard and Grandpa left us. It was an awful day; parting is never easy. But we were all filled with hope. I knew I would miss them, but there was plenty of work to do with the boys, the garden, and the house. Plus, my mother was close by in Neurode.

#

A year went by, I got only two letters from Grandpa, no money. He still had no job, but Greta and Erhard's family were helping him.

One day when I was peeling potatoes a German official came to the door. He wrote down information about where I was born and how long I had lived there. This bothered me and I tried to ask questions. He only assured me it was routine, and I should have registered some time ago. It scared me because now they knew I was alone with the boys. This was not good. The policeman gave me an official paper that was a copy of the information he collected. He told me that it needed to be with me wherever I went. I didn't like it at all, but what could I do?

#

Time passed, posters were up everywhere. Posters about how

bad the Jews were. I noticed one with a picture of the guy Greta and I saw in the town a few years ago. Everyone in the picture was saluting him with outstretched arms. The words read "Hitler Youth (Hitlerjugend und Deutches Jungvolk) Parade. All boys and girls must be there! Gather in the town square at 8 am on Saturday, August 6, 1933."

That was five days away. I had to hatch a plan to keep them from going to the parade. I didn't trust that man. If the boys marched or even attended the event, we might never get to America. I had only a few days to sleep on it. Going to my mother's was out of the question because we would have gotten her caught up in this whole thing. A man hungry for power would not care about reuniting two little boys with their father, he would care about no one but himself.

#

Saturday arrived. The boys stayed in their nightclothes, tucked in bed. I prepared the teakettle, filled it with water and placed it on the stove. I lit the stove at eight o'clock in the morning, expecting that trouble would arrive soon after that. I got two washrags and put them next to the sink, and then went to the boys' bedroom.

"Gisbert and Dietfried, this is very serious. Listen to me," I said in a firm voice that betrayed my worries. "Police will be coming to the house soon, you must act like you are very sick, pretend that you can barely move and say NOTHING until they leave. Do you understand? If you ever want to see your father again, you must do exactly as I say."

I went to the front window and watched, waiting and pacing the floor, always with one eye on the window. My hands shook and I heard my heart pounding in my ears. Trying to convince myself not to be scared, I checked on the boys. Dietfried begged me to let him get up, to go out and play, and to use the bathroom. I let him go only as far as the toilet and watched his every move, knowing how easily he could find mischief. I tucked him back in his bed, feeling a bit relieved. Then I told Gisbert to go use the toilet too. Who knew how long this morning would be?

My faded dress swished as I headed for the front window. Waiting, clenching my shaking hands, anxiety almost overwhelmed me. By the time it was only nine o'clock; it felt like hours had passed. Suddenly, at the end of the street, I saw them. Four men marching in brown shirts and black breeches with black boots that reached their knees.

Setting the washrags in the cold sink I poured the boiling water over them, picked them up and wrung them out, being careful not to burn my hands. I rushed into the boys' room and placed one on each forehead.

"Okay, now they're coming. Remember, not a word, don't move and leave this cloth on your head!" I told the boys.

Just as I hurried out the door of their room, I heard the sound I'd been dreading.

Stomp! Stomp! Stomp! Stomp! Stomp! …boots coming up

my front steps.

"Frau! Open this door immediately!"

A fist pounded on the front of my door. Gritting my teeth and clenching my hands, I took a deep breath, and turned the doorknob.

In they rushed!

"Where are they? You have two sons! They should be at the parade! Where are they?" a handsome one, probably the youngest, shouted in my face.

"They are very ill," I answered in fright trying to keep my voice steady.

I moved to the bedroom ahead of them and snatched up the washrags. One soldier went to Dietfried and another to Gisbert to feel their foreheads. They both jerked their hands away as if bit by dogs.

"Ah, Ya!" The youngest policeman cried as he turned to leave the bedroom.

A horrible red mark stood out on his right temple. It looked like a squashed raspberry. Trying not to stare at it, I looked down at his polished black boots that reflected my face.

"Frau, listen carefully! This time it will be okay; but the next parade or meeting for our Führer, your boys had **better** be there! You do not want to be treated as an enemy of the state. Verstehen Sie (do you understand)?"

"Ya, I understand, and I promise you they will be there. They would be in the parade today if they weren't so sick."

"Heil Hitler!" They saluted with straight arms and marched

down the stairs and back into the street.

I collapsed into the chair in the living room.

Chapter Three

Oklahoma City 1956

I jumped as the front door opened! Grandpa and Annie came in carrying bags of meat from the butcher's, ice, and chicken feed.

"So, what's for dinner?" Grandpa bellowed.

"Wurst, sauerkraut and potatoes" Grandma replied as she bustled about filling pots with water.

"Kennie, what did you do when we were gone?"

"Grandma did stuff like make cream into butter with her Sunbeam Mixmaster. I was like magic! I just sat in the kitchen at the white table and watched her while she told me the best story ever!"

"Really? About what? Was it a fairy tale? Or a story about George Washington or Abe Lincoln?" Annie asked.

"No. It was about this mean, crazy German guy. Grandma didn't trust him so she sent Grandpa and their best friends away to America and the police came to get her and Daddy and Uncle Freddie," I replied.

"Oh Kennie, that's just a made-up story, right Grandpa?" Annie asked.

"Ya. And even if it was true, we wouldn't talk about it. Now let's have dinner," Grandpa said scowling.

Annie and I cleared off the table and put on the tablecloth that Grandma sewed pretty daisies on. We set plates and silverware in front of each chair. Grandma put the wurst on a plate and the potatoes and kraut in big bowls. She poured us each a glass of milk and Annie brought them to the table.

"We even have fresh butter and cottage cheese for our potatoes. Here in America, we are rich! Liebling, you can put it on the table." Grandma smiled as she gave me the bowl.

I pretended the cottage cheese was a small pot of gold and carried it carefully, putting it in the very center of the table.

We all sat down to eat, said a quiet prayer, and enjoyed the good food.

"Ida, why are you telling these little ones about our old problems? They are over. We must forget the old times. We are in America now. We are rich. I have a good job and we have money enough for our house, a big yard, and we'll never go hungry again," Grandpa was almost shouting.

It was then I knew Grandma's story had to be true. I couldn't wait to hear more. But, I had to be alone with Grandma.

Grandma shouted back at Grandpa in German. Even though I didn't know what she was saying, I could tell she was angry.

As soon as Grandpa finished eating, he shoved his chair into the table and stormed out the front door. Annie helped Grandma clear the table and put the dishes in the sink. I was still eating and wanted to be sure to eat every last curd of my cottage cheese.

"Grandma, why was Grandpa so mad?" Annie asked.

"Oh, it's nothing really. He just thinks that we can make bad times go away by pretending they never happened. Instead, they never go away, they just eat away at you and make you mean and miserable, unless you talk about them," Grandma answered.

"Grandma, are you talking about the story you told Kennie?" Annie wanted to know.

"That was only the beginning," Grandma said looking up to the ceiling.

"So Grandma, we insist you tell us more now, while Grandpa is gone. We won't say a word, we promise. PLEASE!" Annie begged.

"Well, okay. But I better make dessert and wash the dishes," Grandma agreed.

Chapter Four

Langenbielau, Germany 1933

Grandma continues her story...

So all day I was worried, knowing it would be only a matter of time before the police came back. That young policeman's serious look and the tone of his voice was enough to convince me that they meant business. The guy with the ugly spot on the side of his face knew more than he could tell me. What if they came back for a surprise visit tomorrow? We couldn't go to my mother's in Neurode, or we'd get her in trouble too, we had no choice but to run. Rumors had it that one could go to the forest, der Wald, and hide in the woods with the Roma; some people called them gypsies. They escaped the government officials and the police because they had no address and the police hated to waste a lot of time with them when they could round up so many more in the cities and towns. Signs were everywhere telling how dirty and bad the Jews were.

It seemed strange to me that the few Jewish people we knew were nice. They kept to themselves, but said hello, went to synagogues and minded their stores. Maybe they were hurting us by cheating us and keeping more money for themselves.

What was I going to do with two little boys? Maybe I was wrong to send my husband to America when we needed him here with us now. Ach! This was not the time for doubts, but for plans and action.

I brushed my long hair and put it into braids, pinned them to the top of my head and put a scarf on. Next I gathered clothes for myself and the boys, stuffed their canvas knapsacks and filled my grocery shopping bag.

My eyes darted around the room catching glimpses of all the things I hated to leave behind, the crystal wine glasses from our wedding day, the family pictures, the dishes, and the furniture Grandpa had made. I had to stop there, had to forget these things. I made myself think about what we would need to survive, our lives depended on it.

Stuffing as much food as I could into our bags, I wondered how long we'd have to survive on it. Gisbert came into the kitchen and our conversation went something like this.

"Mama, What are you doing? You aren't running away without us, are you?" he asked me in the frightened voice of a nine year old.

"No, no I would never do that. You and Dietfried are more important to me than life itself. We three are going on an adventure together."

"When? Can we leave now?" Gisbert wanted to know.

"No, it wouldn't be an adventure unless we left after dark, now would it? Now you go and get your boots and heavy clothes and find Dietfried's too." I told him gently, but firmly.

"You both must stay in the house and be quiet. Don't say anything to Diet just yet, okay? This is very important. Do you understand?" I tried to make Gisbert realize the seriousness of the situation without frightening him.

"Ya," Gisbert nodded.

"Now I must go to the yard and dig up some more potatoes, I said grabbing the small shovel."

Outside, I checked carefully that no one was watching, and I also unlatched the back gate, pouring a little oil in the hinges to be sure it didn't squeak. After digging and gathering up big handfuls of potatoes in my apron I hurried inside.

The boys sat on the floor and played with the little blocks of wood, their 'pretend' cars. The afternoon dragged on, fear and nervousness in my stomach made me feel as if I was going to explode.

The street was quiet, eerie, as the sky became a deep pink and then darkness set in. The boys dressed in layers of clothes; we would need them as it got colder.

My mother would be worried to death when she didn't hear from us by Wednesday. Surely, she would come here. She knew our special hiding place so I wrote a note for her.

Dearest Mama,

I have left with the boys, for fear the police will come back for us. They did not go to the Hitler Youth parade this morning because they were sick. The police came. I will contact you when we are safe.

    Love you always, your Tochter, Ida.

A tear dripped onto the paper. My heart was heavy, knowing I might never see Mama again. But this was no time for crying.

I moved the rug, pushed the molding up, and slid the floorboard. Only a carpenter could make this so invisible. Reaching in, I pulled out the box, took all the money we had and slipped it into my pocket. Carefully, I folded the note, touched it to my lips and kissed it. As soon as the note was in the box, I replaced it in the space, moved the floorboard back, and put the rug in place.

Rumbling! Voices outside! My heart stopped. Quickly I stood up and straightened my skirt. The boys! I rushed into their room, and closed the door.

"Diet and Gis, back in bed! Now!" I said in a loud whisper as I shoved the block "cars" under the bed with my shoe.

Hurrying to the kitchen I checked that the water was still hot and peeked through the curtains, without touching them. There was shouting at the neighbor's front door. Jacob, Rachel and Isaac were being forced out of their house and into a wagon filled with hay. Jacob had a suitcase in his hand. Maybe Isaac didn't march in the parade either, I thought, or maybe the signs about the Jews had something to do with this. Holding my breath and praying, I was praying that we were not next.

Scurrying to hide our bags in the stairwell, and racing back to the window, I saw the Police coming our way. My heart was pounding like it was going to come out of my chest.

Shouts in the street in the darkness made me stretch my eyes to try to figure out what was going on. Faintly, the image of the young policeman with the ugly mark on his face became visible.

"Nein, nicht das Haus. (No, not this house.) The fever… Leave them… Next time, if those boys are missing from our parade…" the policeman's voice trailed off.

They didn't even come toward the steps, but they kept marching past our house.

"Ach! Gott sei Dank!" ("Thank God") I whispered.

Waiting until the street was empty again was not easy. Finally, when there was not a sound, we stacked our things by the back door and Diet whined that he was hot and hungry. I gave the boys each a piece of bread and leaned down to talk to them.

"It's dark and we are going on a great adventure. You must be strong and silent. We need to stay together, so I am going to tie this rope to each of our wrists. That way we won't get lost in the dark. We are going out the back gate, past the park to the old long road to the Bauer's farm. If you hear any sound, freeze. That is part of the adventure game. Do you both understand?" I asked the boys.

"But where are we going? When will we be coming home?"

Diet planted his feet firmly on the floor as if demanding answers.

"Don't worry, you'll have to wait and see. Just stay with me and be quiet as we walk," I told him.

Chapter Five

Oklahoma City 1956

Listening so hard to Grandma's story, I never saw Annie lick the bowl or Grandma put the cake in the oven. Now, mmm... the chocolate cake smelled so good. When it was all done baking, Grandma took the pans out of the oven and put the bottom layer on a big round plate. She tipped the other layer out of the pan onto a small rack. Then she mixed the icing in her Sunbeam Mixmaster.

"Okay girls, let's leave the cake to cool and then we can put icing on it. Why don't you go watch for Grandpa?" Grandma said.

We rushed to the front window and looked for the blue Nash. We saw a neighbor walking up the street and a black car drove by.

"Annie, do you believe Grandma's story now?" I asked her.

"Um, I don't know. But we don't want any trouble so remember don't say a word about it when Grandpa gets here," Annie replied.

"My lips are zipped." I said as I moved my pointer finger across my mouth.

Grandma was still in the kitchen cleaning up and icing the

cake. She wiped her face with her apron. Maybe she was crying, and that's why she sent us out of the room. I wondered if she ever saw her mother again. She got away from the mean policemen and made it to America, or she wouldn't be here today.

"Crunch!" the wheels on the blue Nash pulled into the yard.

"Grandpa's home now! Can we have dessert?" Annie shouted back to the kitchen, so Grandma could hear her.

"Yes, you girls can put little plates and forks on the table now. And remember, not a word about our secret story," Grandma whispered.

"Grandpa! Grandpa! Grandma made us a chocolate cake for dessert!" I said as I ran to open the door for him.

"Ahhh, yes, I can smell it! Mmm, let's sit down and eat. I have just enough time before I go to work at the bank," Grandpa said.

"Grandpa, how come you go to work when the bank is closed?" Annie asked.

"I guard all the money at night and clean the floors when there's no one there to make them dirty," he answered.

As soon as Grandpa left and we heard the car pull away, Annie and I rushed to Grandma and helped clear the table.

"Grandma, you can tell us more of the story now that Grandpa's gone. Where did you go on your adventure?" Annie wanted to know.

"Was it fun? Or scary?" I asked.

"Okay, my little ones, but only until bedtime." Grandma told us.

Our heads were full of questions as we sat back down at the kitchen table.

Chapter Six

Langenbielau, Germany 1933

Grandma's story continues…

It was a long night, but luckily not a cold one. I tried to keep a slow even pace, staying in the shadows, as we made our way out of our little town and onto the country road. We froze when a man on a bicycle rode past on the other side of the street. He seemed not to notice us as he kept up his own pace. Maybe he was in a hurry to get wherever he was going. It was good that he didn't even slow down or turn his head in our direction.

I held my breath until he was completely out of sight. The boys were good and they stayed still waiting for me to move again. It seemed like we'd been walking for hours, but the Bauer's farm was only a few miles out of town. When we got close to it, a dog was barking in the distance. We didn't dare stop there.

"How much longer? I'm tired. I want to go to bed. I hate this adventure!" Diet whispered.

"Shhh! Not now, Diet, we must keep going," I replied trying to be patient with him.

"This is no fun!" Diet continued.

"Shhh!" I repeated and pulled Diet closer to me, with my arm around his shoulders.

The barking sounded closer.

My hope was that the dog was on the farm and not a police dog.

My heart started to pound harder. Looking for places to hide in the brush near the side of the road, we three trudged along. Our coats were dark so that gave us some protection. We kept moving along.

The boys were tired; so was I. When would it be safe to stop? We had to push on as far as we could. Our ultimate goal was safety in America.

Diet stopped and sat down in the dirt.

"I know, Diet, you can go on no longer. We'll stop soon, but first we must find a nice spot in the woods, so cars won't be able to spot us." I sounded as if I had a frog in my throat.

"Ach! Finally, I thought we were going to keep going until we collapsed. I'm hungry, thirsty and tired, too," Gisbert said.

Slowly I moved through the fallen branches and leaves. It had been so quiet that our feet crunching and rustling in the brush sounded like a thousand squirrels chasing each other. We came to a large fallen tree and Gisbert and I helped Diet over it. We untied the rope that had kept us together for our long walk. Straining my eyes in the dark, I made my way back to the road and covered our trail, then

Gisbert and I climbed over the tree. Diet was nowhere to be seen. Two minutes of freedom and he had wandered off. That child always made me worry.

"He can't be very far," Gisbert said.

But in the dark, he'd be hard to find.

"Diet, Diet, come, I'm making us a wonderful soft bed of fallen leaves," I whispered as loud as I dared.

We were still, listening for a hint of where he might have gone. The sound of water running caught my attention. Moving toward the water, I saw the outline of a small boy with his back to me. Diet was peeing. As soon as he was done, I rushed over and grabbed him. We made a cozy spot behind the fallen tree and fell fast asleep close together. When we reached the Bauer's farm it was surrounded by police and there were at least two dogs. It was too dangerous to go anywhere near it. So we followed the corn rows at the edge of the back pastures.

Our days were spent huddled in spots that were out of sight of the roads, and our nights brought us up and down steep hills, deeper into the woods. We hadn't seen a real person in days and we were almost out of food. The sound of every car on the road made me jump, even when I was asleep. The boys adjusted well to this adventure, even though it wasn't the fun they expected. A jug of milk and a warm bath would have been wonderful, but we had to press on. I lost track of the days and worried about where we'd find more food. You didn't know who to trust in that crazy world, but soon I had to find someone to help us or we'd starve to death.

Diet did his share of whining, especially climbing the hills. Some days I wondered if we were still in Germany or if we'd crossed over the Czech border.

#

One morning I was looking for a safe place to stop for the day when I heard people talking, human voices and noises in a clearing up ahead. Making sure the boys were behind me, I put my finger in front of my lips, hid behind a tree and peeked around it to see six or eight men and women and a few little kids around a crude shelter covered with branches. They were hiding too. The smell of cooked meat made my mouth water.

Should I stop and talk to them? Ask them for food? They hardly have enough for themselves, I'm sure. What will they do to us? Hurt us or help us? If they are afraid that we'll squeal on them and let the police know they are here, we'll never escape. We must be careful.

They were laughing as we approached on tiptoe. Trying to get a closer look would help me decide if they might be friends or enemies.

"Ach! What have we here? Three rag-tags on the run?" a gruff voice from the tallest of the men came our way.

Everyone stopped and looked at us.

"Hello!" I said, barely able to speak.

"So what are you doing here? Can we help you?" the tall man

asked.

"Yes, I hope you can give us something to eat," I replied.

"Ach! This is your lucky day! We caught porcupine and two squirrels yesterday. But we share only if you give us something," the leader of the group said.

"So what can we give you?" I asked.

"Your story. We need to know what's happening out there, and we don't dare leave the safety of the forest," was the reasonable request from the tall one.

"I'm afraid I don't know much myself," I answered truthfully.

"But surely it's more than we know. You can start with your name and I take it these two fellows are your kids, Ya?" the leader continued.

"I'm Ida and these are my sons, Dietfried and Gisbert. We come from a small village near Reichenbach. My boys were sick the day of a big Hitler youth parade. The police came in the morning demanding to know why they weren't there. If I hadn't let them in, I'm certain they would have battered in the front door. Later in the evening, just about dusk, the police were back on our street. They took away the Jewish family in a hay wagon. We didn't stay around to wait for them to come back for us. This one officer had a strange mark on his temple. He told the rest to move on when they started toward our house."

"Yeah, this guy had a red mark that looked like a squished berry right here," Diet added pointing to his temple using his index finger like a gun. "It was weird when he came over and felt my forehead to see if I had a fever."

"Anything else?" the tall one wanted to know.

"We found a piece of newspaper on the road. It said that Adolf Hitler is now Chancellor of Germany," I added.

"Ach du Himmel! Bad news! That man is out to get us along with the Jews. He hates Romas. So we must be even more careful," the leader of the group was upset.

"Okay, okay, enough big people talk. Can we eat now?" Dietfried asked.

"But, of course. You must be very hungry," the tall one said as he patted Diet on the head.

Two women scurried about the camp and brought out a pot with onions, mushrooms and some meat in it.

"Sorry, it's cold. We eat early in the morning when the food is hot, since we let it cook all night in a pit," one of the women said.

"Why?" Diet asked.

"Fires make smoke, my lad, and smoke rises, so it can be seen in the daytime. At night, it's not so risky."

The boys dug in. Trying to be polite was really hard. We hadn't had cooked food since we left Langenbielau.

As soon as Diet had filled his little stomach, he was off exploring. He came back with a piece of a broken clay pot.

"Too bad this broke," he said waving it around.

"My lad, we broke it on purpose," the tall one told him.

"Huh, why'd you do that?" Diet persisted.

"To get the porcupine meat out. Look here. When we coated the animal in clay, all the quills got stuck in it, so when we broke the cooked clay we didn't have to separate the meat from the quills. See, this soil is mostly clay over here. That's where we got it, and the pit here is where we cooked the porcupine all night, so it's nice and tender," the tall one explained.

It had a strange flavor, but it was meat and we really needed the nourishment.

Gisbert finally had something to say. "The mushrooms are good. But aren't some poisonous?"

"Ya, but you have to be smart and know how to pick the good ones, " the leader told him.

"Will you teach me to tell them apart?" Gisbert asked the tall one.

"But of course. When you are done eating. We'll have to do a bit of hiking since we've already picked most of the mushrooms close by."

Diet looked sleepy and I was exhausted. I think this was the first time I'd relaxed since we left the house. A kind lady seemed to read my mind and told us to come inside the hut and get a good rest. Gisbert went off in search of mushrooms, while Diet and I used our packs as pillows and slept soundly.

When I woke up, it was dark. Looking around, I saw little Diet still sleeping. I came out of the shelter and smelled a fire. In the dim light I saw everyone except the tall man and Gisbert. My heart stopped.

"Where are Gisbert and the tall one?" I needed to know.

"We're not sure. Albert is usually back by dark," the kind lady said.

My voice must have betrayed my fears. She came over and put an arm on my shoulder.

"It's not likely that they ran into trouble, and even if they did, Albert is the best person to be with. He's a clever one, you know," the kind one reassured me.

I was glad Diet was still sleeping, and in the shelter. It was getting colder and I couldn't help but worry. Should I have trusted them? Did they get caught? Gisbert never got instructions on what to do, what to say, to deny everything. How could I have been so stupid? If anything happened to him, I never would have forgiven myself. What would I have told his father? ...if I ever saw him again.

Chapter Seven

Oklahoma City 1956

"Ach! Girls, it's so late, I must get you to bed quickly. Grandpa will be home soon! Brush your teeth and put on your PJs now," Grandma told us as she motioned toward the bathroom.

We did as Grandma said, knowing the stories would end if Grandpa caught us awake. Annie and I rushed to our beds and pulled up our sheets. We could pretend, even if we were not really asleep when Grandpa got home.

"Annie, do you believe Grandma's stories now?" I whispered.

"Well, I don't know. She and Grandpa speak German and Polish. But I could never imagine Mommy sending Daddy away and staying in a place that's not safe with us. Besides, you don't believe that Grandma, Daddy and Uncle Freddie lived in the forest, like in the fairy tales, do you?" Annie asked.

"It happened a long, long time ago. So maybe real people did live in the forest. There was a war then so maybe families did get separated. I'm sure Grandma's story is true," I insisted.

"Is not."

"Is too."

"Is not."

"Cruuunch!"we heard the gravel under the car tires.

"Shhh! Grandpa's home." Annie whispered.

I closed my eyes, pretending I was asleep.

#

The light shined through the curtains. It had to be morning, but I was still so sleepy. Annie's bed was empty. Did she really go away mushroom hunting or was I dreaming?

Annie and Grandma came into the bedroom and called me "Sleepyhead."

"It's a pretty day, and Grandpa put fresh water in your wading pool this morning, so you girls should put on your swimsuits and go outside after breakfast," Grandma told us.

"Where were you, Annie? Did you go mushroom hunting?" I asked.

"What? Of course not, I was in the bathroom, Silly," Annie said.

We were sitting in the pool under the pretty mimosa tree with its fluffy pink flowers and the smell of petunias was all around us.

"I wish there were other kids here for us to play with." Annie said.

"It's okay, I wish we could go inside and see what Grandpa is doing. He's always making something neat like that great big chalkboard in his workshop. When he's not working, he hides in the puzzle room. That's even more fun. In the cool, dark corner of the basement his card table always has a partly-done jigsaw puzzle on it. A bare bulb hangs from the ceiling giving plenty of light," I explained.

"How can you find that fun?" Annie asked, "Besides, Grandma says we need the sunshine."

Even splashing in the water, it was hot out that day. Grandma called us inside and told us to get dressed to go shopping with her. We hurried inside, dried ourselves off, and changed into our striped short sets. We almost matched, except Annie's was blue, mine was orange, and hers was bigger, of course. We got in the back seat of the blue Nash and Grandma sat behind the steering wheel. First, it was off to the Piggly-Wiggly. What a funny name for a grocery store. We liked it because they had a playground, so we could ride the swings while Grandma got the groceries. A lady with long hair stood at the gate and made sure everyone was safe. After Grandma got the groceries and came back for us, we went to the butcher's where Grandma bought sausages and stew meat. Last, we went to the dairy farm and Grandma gave them the big empty milk jug and they gave her a new one that was full to the brim, with milk on the bottom and thick cream on top.

Home again we went. Grandma put everything away and I sneaked downstairs to find Grandpa. He was cutting some wood to make a cabinet, like the drawing on the blackboard with all the numbers scribbled on the sides. When he saw me, he stopped and grinned.

"Ach, I guess it's time for me to take a break and work on the puzzle with Kliene Kenda." Grandpa said as he took my hand and guided me past the pieces of wood and sawdust on the floor.

We sat on stools at the card table. The pieces were all sorted and most of the border was done, so I looked for the flat pieces and Grandpa started working on the barn. Every time I found a piece, he laughed and smiled at me. I loved being in our little hideaway.

#

"Oh! There you are!" Annie shouted as she came carefully through the workshop.

"Ach! You must go before we both get in trouble with Grandma!" Grandpa said.

I got off my stool and followed Annie through the workshop and up the stairs.

"Liebling, what were you doing?" Grandma asked the minute she saw me.

"I just went down to Grandpa's workshop. He's making a new cabinet out of the prettiest wood." I said, hoping she would be okay with that and Annie didn't tell on me.

"Can we hear more of the story of Gisbert getting lost when Grandpa leaves?" Annie asked.

Heavy steps came up the stairs, so we didn't get an answer from Grandma.

"So, what are you going to do this afternoon?" Grandma asked Grandpa.

"We need chicken feed, so I'll go out to the Farmers Co-op Store and I'll be back in time for dinner," he said as he grabbed the keys off the hook and headed out the door.

The second the door shut, Annie repeated her question.

"Yes, I guess so. My, I had no idea what I started when I told a little of my story to Kennie, but I suppose I can't leave you hanging now," Grandma said.

We hurried to the sparkling clean kitchen table, and sat down.

Chapter Eight

In the Forest 1933-34

Grandma continues…

So, it turned to night and still no sign of Albert and
Gisbert. I cuddled close to Diet in the shelter, but couldn't sleep a
wink.

My mind raced, awful thoughts were creeping in. What if they
were captured? What if Gisbert was hauled away in a wagon filled
with straw to some horrible work camp? Should I have trusted
Albert? Did Albert send Gisbert into a dangerous place? Will the
mushroom hunters come back? When? Are they alone? Where *are*
they?

All night I wondered and the agony of not knowing the
whereabouts of my oldest son was enough to make me crazy. A bit of
light came through the trees and I realized it was morning. There was
chatter among the gypsies, the children were running around and Diet
was with them, playing with sticks. It was hard to get my tired body
up off the dirt floor, but I managed to get up and dust off my skirt. It
was so cold you could see your breath. I asked the others what they

thought happened.

Of course, no one had a clue. They gathered what little food there was, and brought it into the hut. We each took a handful and tried hard to eat one small bite at a time to make it last.

"Shh!" one of the Romas whispered loudly.

We heard rustling in the distance. My heart leaped, as I jumped up and peered out in the direction of the noise. There was nothing there, no one. But I kept watching. The kind one came over to watch with me. Then I made out three figures coming toward us. Did this mean trouble?

Soon we could see Albert, Gisbert and another skinny boy. As they got closer, we saw that their pants legs and shoes were all wet. I rushed over and hugged Gisbert.

Quickly, we brought them into the shelter. The sleeves of a shirt were tied into knots and the strange boy put it on the tree stump in the center of the hut. Albert untied the sleeves with his big hands around the edges; he laid out potatoes, eggs, and mushrooms. Everyone stared in amazement at all the food.

"Where did you get all this?" the kind one asked.

Albert and the boy took off their shoes and peeled off dripping wet socks. Gisbert's boots were torn and he took them off and then wrung out his socks. We wrapped their feet and legs in cloths and blankets as they took off their wet pants, too.

"When we were out hunting mushrooms, this boy, Joshua, came running from a road," Gisbert said pointing to the skinny boy.

Albert continued, "He had jumped off the back of a cart and had wandered for a few days where he found a farm. He sneaked into the barn at night and found sacks of potatoes in the loft, so he took some. The chickens were all inside on perches, so he slipped outside to the chicken yard and collected all the eggs he could find in the moonlight. Being smart, he put straw between the eggs to keep them from breaking. Then he heard dogs barking, so he took off for the woods, scared that the police were on to him, or maybe the farmer. We had collected all of these mushrooms and were just about to turn back, since it was already dark. When we saw Joshua coming toward us, we froze, thinking at first that he was out to get us. But soon we realized that he was running too and he offered us the shirt full of food.

We started heading in the direction of the camp, following a crisscross path to keep those dogs confused. But that took us most of the night. The dogs seemed closer, then further away and closer again. We knew we had to lose them before daylight, so I took us to a shallow part of the stream. We waded across. The dogs were nearer to us again. I knew we'd lose our scent in the water, but we needed to be quiet and hidden on the other side, so we went way upstream and pretty far from the water, where we found a deep gully. There we covered ourselves with branches and leaves and huddled together for what seemed like hours," Albert explained.

"Finally, when I was sure it was safe for us to proceed, we rubbed our feet and trudged back here," Albert finished.

"Wow! Gisbert had a real adventure," Dietfried shouted, "wish I could have gone too."

"Well, it's about time for us to be moving on." I told them.

"Not before we are sure Gisbert's feet are okay and we'll make a big pot of soup and check our traps today. You can leave tomorrow night. But where will you go?" Albert asked.

"We must get to Hamburg; my sister, Minne, is there." I replied.

"So, how will you find your way?" asked Albert.

"I don't really know, you are never sure…"

Chapter Nine

Oklahoma City 1956

Grandma stopped her story as the door opened. Grandpa was home.

"What are you doing? I thought you wanted the girls outside in the sunshine?" after these questions, he muttered something in Polish.

Grandma cut him off "I suppose you got the chicken feed. I'll run out and open the gates for you."

Uh oh! Grandpa knew what was going on!

"Okay, just in case he asks again, here's what we tell Grandpa. We were playing a guessing game, like we do in the car. You know, the one where you start with A, then B, C and so on, giving names of a woman, her husband, where they live and what they eat. We only came in a little while ago to cool off since it was so hot outside. Got it?" Annie said.

"Yes," I answered.

When Grandpa came in, he got cleaned up while Grandma fixed sour red cabbage in the pressure cooker and meat in the bottom drawer of her stove. She called it a broiler. It was easy to see why she was chubby since she loved to cook and eat. The kitchen was her favorite place in the whole world, even though it was always so hot in there.

We couldn't wait until Grandpa went to work so we'd be able to hear more of the Diet and Gisbert story from Grandma. We listened to Grandpa talk about the bank, how boring. It seemed to take forever to finish eating and clearing the dishes. Finally Grandpa left for work.

"Okay, Grandma, did you get to Hamburg? How did you know which way to go? Where did you get food?" Annie asked.

"Haven't you two heard enough for one day?" Grandma replied.

"No, no, tell us more... PLEEZE, PLEEZE." Annie and I pleaded.

Chapter Ten

On the Way to Mannheim 1934

Grandma continues...

Joshua, the skinny boy, finally spoke. "I know a place where you will be safe on the way. My town, Mannheim is a few weeks away. There is a kindly shoemaker there in the center of town, who's not Jewish. His name is Alfons. I know he will help you. People come from far away to get special shoes for crippled children from him. Lots of shabby-looking folks come there and no one thinks anything of it. ...I'm sorry, I don't mean to insult you, but you don't exactly look well-dressed."

"So how do we get to Mannheim?" I asked.

"You want to travel west, so the sun is at your back in the morning and you are walking toward it in the afternoon. If you follow the Rhein River and stay near the trains when you can; they will shield you from sight and the noise will help to hide your movements." Joshua replied.

"So how far is it?" I asked.

"Hmm, about three weeks to Mannheim, I'd say." Joshua said

slowly, as if thinking hard about his answer.

"Eat before you leave and we can give you a few cooked eggs, a potato or two and some mushrooms, but you know we don't have much," The kind Roma said.

"We could never thank you enough for all your help." I said sincerely.

"Mama, do we have to leave? Why? I have friends here. And don't tell me about another adventure! I don't wanna go!" Diet fussed.

"We have no choice, Dietfried. Some day you will understand. Now come," I said firmly.

"Waaa! Nien, nein, nein!!" Diet protested.

"Ach! Mein Kind! Your father is waiting for us," I replied beginning to lose my patience.

"When will we see him?" Diet whined.

"Soon, now let's be on our way," and I grabbed his hand.

Although I knew we had to move on, it was hard to leave. These people were kind to us. We would have starved and been half dead by now if not for them.

We all said our goodbyes and thanks, and started on the way.

After a few days, Gisbert was limping.

"What's the matter? Did you slip or twist your ankle?" I asked him, with concern painted on my face.

"No, my feet are sore from being frozen when we crossed the water to get away with Joshua. My boots were tight and the water came through the cracks in them."

"Well we must push on. In a bit, we'll rest and you can change socks. We are lucky that Joshua told us about the good shoemaker in Mannheim," I said.

#

We managed to walk and walk until we could move no more. Then we found a wooded spot with tall blueberry bushes. Although the berries were long gone, it made a nice place to hide for the night. We had been lucky, the weather warmed a bit and we hadn't had any rain or snow.

We lost track of the days, and I had no idea where we were. As we came near a city an old gentleman in a black topcoat came across the road toward us. I dared to talk to him. We needed to know where we were. His white beard, drooping head and dusty shoes made it evident that he could not be part of the police force who came to our house. As he got closer, his dark brown eyes reflected sorrow and he looked as if he was going to burst into tears at any moment.

"Good day," he said in a robot-like voice.

"Good day to you. Where are you going?" I replied.

"Don't rightly know. I've just been dismissed from my job at the University here in Heidelberg," the old man said.

"Ach, so this is Heidelberg. Now what happened? Why?" I asked, since I couldn't begin to understand.

"Don't rightly know. The Nazis don't like us. It matters not how well we do our jobs or what we know. They think we are not good for Germany. They say awful things that are not true and put up

posters to defame us. It's terrible and I have a feeling there is more to
come. But I shouldn't say too much," the man explained with
disappointment, and then he asked "Where are you going?"

"To Mannheim, to get special shoes made for my son. We had
no idea it would be such a long journey. Is there some place where
we might get food and rest?" I asked.

"So, where are you coming from?" he wanted to know.

"A tiny village near Reichenbach," I replied.

"Ach! Such a long journey! Maybe the baker can help you.
His family is from there too," the kindly gentleman told me.

"Are you sure it will be safe for us to go there?" I asked.

"No one is safe for certain anymore. But the baker is kind and
honorable and so is his wife. Follow this road and go right on
Hauptstrasse. You can smell the bakery and don't be afraid to go in,"
the old gentleman instructed me.

"Danke and good luck to you," I replied, grateful for his help.

#

We went on our way and before we came to the street, we
took off our coats, and shook them out trying to make sure there were
no leaves or briars on them. It was important not to look too much
like ragamuffins. Checking in my bag for the money we brought, I
was sure we could buy a loaf of bread. We got to the Hauptstrasse
and found the bakery by following the smell. When we got near the
door, I saw police inside. My hand reached out for Diet's shoulder
and I steered him around the corner, put my index finger over my

lips, and Gisbert followed. He had a good sense for danger and yet could look as if he hadn't a care in the world. I watched for the Polizei to walk out, praying they wouldn't see us.

Phew, they headed in the opposite direction, as they laughed and joked around. One spoke loudly about Dachau, where they sent political enemies. It must be a bad place to go, I thought, from what I could hear of their conversation. As soon as the police were out of sight, we went into the bakery.

The smell of fresh bread was like heaven. I took a deep breath and smiled.

"Good morning! We are on a long journey and would like a loaf of bread," I said.

"But, of course. Which one?" the nice man replied, happy to be of service.

"This large one here, and could we trouble you for a place to wash up?" I asked.

"I…uh..." the baker hesitated, "suppose."

"Annelise, could you take the Frau and her two little boys to the back room?" he called to the lady in the kitchen, probably his wife.

A chubby woman came out from the room where the oven was, looked down at Diet and smiled.

"Such a cute little one, what's your name?"

Diet looked at me to be sure it was okay.

I nodded and said, "go ahead and tell the nice lady your

name."

Diet stood tall, with his shoulders back, and reached out his hand saying, "I'm Dietfried, and I'm pleased to meet you! Now can I wash my hands so Mama will let me eat?"

"Of course, Dietfried!" Annelise laughed.

She showed us to a small washroom. We cleaned our hands and faces, went back into the front of the bakery and found a small table in the corner away from the window.

Thanking Annelise, I paid for our bread.

She asked where we were staying.

My reply was that we didn't have a lot of money and couldn't afford a room, because we were on our way to get special shoes for my son in Mannheim. The shoes would cost a lot. It was pretty obvious that we were really tired from our long journey. Although I didn't exactly ask, I hoped she'd offer to let us stay with them for the night.

Annelise went to the front of the store and waited on a few more customers. It would have been wonderful to stay there forever; the bakery was warm and smelled delicious. Then I heard her talking in a quiet voice to her husband and he peeked around the corner. He said something about not looking like Jews and then nodded his head. I held my breath and prayed.

Annelise came back and said it would be okay for us to stay, but just for the night. The boys would have to sleep on the floor, and I could use the couch. A wave of relief overwhelmed me. She told us that we could wash ourselves and our clothes after we ate and Annelise even gave us some hot tea to drink with our bread. I thanked her again.

As soon as we were all clean for the first time in forever, I offered to help in any way we could. Dietfried curled up on the couch and fell fast asleep. Gisbert swept the floor and moved with his legs so stiff I knew his feet really hurt. Washing up the mixing bowls and cleaning off the countertops kept me busy. The day went by and we closed down the bakery for the night. Annelise made soup with beets, carrots, potatoes and onions. She even served butter with the bread. It was delicious! The boys wolfed down their food as if they hadn't eaten in months; actually they hadn't had a real meal like this in so long. With blankets on the floor, the boys went to sleep as soon as it was dark. Trying to show my appreciation, I helped to wash the dishes and mop the kitchen floor. The couch was so comfortable, I had forgotten how nice it was to go to sleep like a real human being!

#

Clanging pots and loud voices woke me up. Where was I? It was still dark or maybe the windows were covered to keep the light out. Slowly, I put my feet on the cold floor and made my way to the window. Pulling aside the heavy curtain, there was a stillness before dawn. Then I saw the outlines of four men in the street by the lamp. They were all standing straight like giant tree trunks. Polizei! My heart pounded. Leaving here might not be so easy I thought. Timing would be everything.

In the small room, I washed my face and pulled our clothes down off the lines where I had hung them after washing last night. I used a tiny drop of the perfume on the shelf, such a luxury to smell nice. After dressing in my clean clothes, I gathered our things and began to pack them up in our bags, which were looking shabby. Some of the dirt and dust came off when I wiped them with a damp cloth. Now our bags looked a little better.

Annelise came into the room.

"I thought I heard someone stirring in here. It's good that you are awake. Even though we know you are not Jews and you aren't in trouble with the law, we think it best that you be ready to leave before the police come. They watch for our lights in the store and come in a half hour later for breakfast. We must serve them whatever they want and they never pay. When you hear them coming, you must go out the back door. We don't want any questions from them or any trouble for you. They have a way of twisting what people say and then the story is entirely different. The last thing I want is for you and the boys to get hauled away in a cart. They are nice kids, especially that Gisbert, sweeping my floor even with his broken feet. I'm sorry to make you get the boys up, but I hope you understand," Annelise explained.

"Yes, I do and thank you again so very much," I replied sincerely.

Shaking the boys, I whispered for them to get up.

"Uhh?!" Diet moaned.

Gisbert rubbed his eyes and leaned up on one elbow.

"Listen boys, you need to go to the bathroom, wash up and be ready to leave. Your knapsacks are ready, we will leave very soon out the back door," I told them.

Annelise came back. She pulled two large loaves of bread wrapped in a towel from under her apron.

"Here take these with you. As soon as you hear noise in the bakery, slip quietly out this door here and go to the left. Follow the street in the opposite direction from which you came, but stay behind the shops and houses. When it ends take the long road to the right and follow it for 17 or 18 kilometers and you'll be in Mannheim. I'll keep the police here as long as I can. Be careful and God bless," Annelise directed us.

"I can't thank you enough for all you've done," I said.

"You would have done the same for us, I'm sure," she replied.

"Annelise, come, they will be here any minute!" The baker called.

Picking up the blankets, I folded them, and left them on the couch. Then I took the large wooden bar off the back door and put it carefully to the side, making sure everything was ready for us to sneak out.

Diet put on his knapsack and I put the warm bread in the top of my bag. It was hard not to break off a piece and eat it, but I didn't want to be distracted. Besides, I needed to save it until we were really hungry.

Boots came stomping up the street. Every muscle in my body tensed up. Pound, pound, pound …fists hit the bakery door.

Quickly, I pushed the back door open and shoved Gisbert and Diet out into the early morning light. My shaking hands pulled the door shut. I grabbed Diet's hand and whispered for Gisbert to take his other one. We made our way down behind the shops and houses.

A dog barked. We froze. Then nothing. The town was still asleep, except for the people in the bakery. One step in front of the other, I led the boys. A twig snapped under my foot. We all jumped, hoping nobody heard. We stood there tense, unable to move. When I realized that all was clear, a huge sigh of relief came out of my mouth. Silently, we moved on.

#

Finally we made it to the edge of town. The sun was almost up over the mountains. We felt safer on the road. Still, I wondered if the police were at all suspicious, if they asked Annelise a lot of questions, if they went into the back and found the wooden bar off the door. The baker and his wife were such nice people, and they asked nothing from us. They didn't deserve any trouble. But both of them seemed clever and they knew those policemen, so I thought they were probably all right.

As we trudged along the road, we listened for cars and ducked into the underbrush whenever we heard any coming. Gisbert complained that his feet hurt and his boots were tight and rubbing his toes. We found a clearing where we couldn't be seen from the road and sat on the ground. I pulled out a loaf of bread and we tore off pieces. It was still a little warm and tasted so good. We all wished we could have curled up and napped there, but we had to keep going. If we were lucky, we'd make it to the shoemaker's before dark.

Chapter Eleven

Oklahoma City 1956

I missed Mommy and Daddy and thought about the bedtime stories they used to read to us, but the stories of Gisbert and Dietfried were even better.

"Don't you think Grandma's stories are better than the ones Mommy and Daddy used to read to us?" I whispered to Annie.

She didn't answer. She could have been asleep, or maybe she was faking because she didn't want to talk to me.

#

When I woke up, it was Saturday. Grandpa didn't go to work. We spent all morning outside. We even brought our peanut butter and jelly sandwiches out and sat on the steps. At home, I always liked weekends, but here it meant no more Gisbert and Diet stories.

"Okay, girls, you need to go down to the basement." Grandma told us.

Hurray! I went straight to the back of Grandpa's workshop to work on the puzzle. It was dark and I couldn't reach the string to turn on the light bulb.

"Annie, come help me!" I called from the dark space.

"No, not now. Why would Grandma want us in the basement? She's always telling us to get outside," Annie questioned.

"I don't know, but I need you to turn on the light…please," I said, trying not to whine.

"Kennie, you can be such a pest. Don't you want to know what's going on?"

"Not really, I just want to work on the puzzle."

"Okay, okay." Annie made her way into Grandpa's puzzle room. She reached her hand out in the dark to find the string and pulled on it. She turned briskly and headed back up the stairs.

As soon as the light came on, I climbed up on my stool and get lost in the puzzle.

"Ah! Look at all the pieces you've found!" Grandpa's voice made me jump.

I hadn't even heard him come in. He sat down on the stool opposite from me and we added pieces to the sky and the flower garden. It was peaceful and cool there, but I still wondered why we were asked to stay in the basement.

#

Grandma cooked a wonderful dinner of chicken, mashed potatoes, gravy, and string beans. Annie and I put on the tablecloth and set the table. We all sat down to eat. Mmm…the food tasted as good as it smelled, and Grandma's gravy dripped over the edge of my pile of buttery, smooth potatoes when I put my fork into them. This was my favorite meal.

Annie finished her vegetables, but picked at her meat and left most of it on the plate. Grandma and Grandpa both asked her what was wrong. She said that maybe she ate too many potatoes, and her tummy didn't feel good. The chicken was delicious; I couldn't believe that she didn't want it. Annie went to lie down on the couch and I helped Grandma with the dishes.

The rest of the day was boring; TV was stupid, just big people shows. Annie wouldn't play with me. The only thing I could do was read a book. When I finished *The Princess and the Pea,* I went to the front window and watched people walk down the street. I looked at what they were wearing and tried to guess if they were friends or how they were related to each other.

It was bedtime and no Gisbert and Diet story cause Grandpa was home. Why wouldn't he let us talk about it?

"Liebling, time for your bath." Grandma called.

At least it was something to do and I loved making suds in the big deep tub with the funny feet. That day was almost over and I couldn't wait to crawl in between my cool cotton sheets.

I hoped Annie wasn't sick.

"Annie, what's the matter? Are you sick?" I whispered when we finally got into bed.

"Not really, but it was awful," she whispered back.

"What?" I wanted to know.

"Well, you know the chickens Grandma has in the back yard?

"

"Of course," I answered.

"When you were busy with the puzzle, I watched Grandma out the back door. You know how she always hates us being in the basement in the daytime, I had to know why she told us to go there today. Here's what I saw. She went out and got a chicken from the pen and did something to it so that it was running around the yard without a head! It was really gruesome. Then when it finally plopped down in a heap, she dunked it into the big pot of boiling water that Grandpa carried out in the yard for her. Then she pulled off all the feathers, and put them, and some other stuff in a bucket that Grandpa took to the compost pile. She brought in the chicken and that's what you ate for dinner! Yuck, I just couldn't even think of eating it." Annie explained.

"So, that's why Grandma told us to get in the basement; she didn't want us to see what she was doing. That's why she never buys chicken at the butcher shop. Now I know why you didn't want to eat it. But it really did taste good." I told Annie.

"I guess killing a chicken and turning it into dinner is no big deal to Grandma, after eating porcupine and starving. But it's pretty yucky to me." Annie said.

#

A few days passed and finally Grandpa was off to work again. Annie and I sat at the kitchen table with milk and gingerbread Kuchen, while Grandma sipped her coffee.

"Tell us more of the Diet and Gisbert story, please Grandma."

"Okay, now where were we?"

"On the road to Mannheim." Annie answered.

Chapter Twelve

Mannheim 1934

Grandma continues…

Ah, yes, we were quietly eating when we heard car after car pass on the road. I counted six or seven in a row. This made me uneasy, so I motioned to the boys to come closer and we moved deeper into the underbrush. Sitting still for a while felt good, but we had to get going again. We waited a little longer to be sure we heard no more cars and made our way back to the road. It was still pretty early in the morning, so we kept walking on. Soon there were farmers in the fields and only a few trees.

Now we had walked as if we knew exactly where we were going. Soon we passed by a small house, made of dark wood with red shutters. We had be careful not to arouse any suspicion. I thought up a story about why we were going to Mannheim that I could tell anyone who might stop us. Gisbert was limping a little with each step, so that made it believable. I tried to watch the house and road both at the same time. A curtain fluttered in the window, but I couldn't be sure if it was the wind or someone watching us. We passed by as quickly as we could, hoping we were not noticed.

Little by little, we put more and more distance between us and the bakery; I could only hope we were going the right way. The sun was coming up over my right shoulder, but the road twisted and turned, so sometimes it was behind us and sometimes in front of us. It was hard to stay aware of every sound and every movement. But I had to know if someone was coming. In those days you never knew who you could trust.

The time went by and we had no idea how long we had been trudging along. The boys were both getting tired, so we counted steps to keep them from complaining. I told Diet how smart he was to be able to count so high. When we got to 100, we started over. A car came from behind us and we just kept walking. I held my breath until it passed. The boys were right about this boring trek; it was not a good adventure. If we didn't get to Mannheim that day, surely we'd be there the next. I thought it would be okay for us to stop on the edge of a field and eat a little more. When I told the boys we could stop, Diet jumped up and down, and did a little dance moving his arms and legs in every direction. In the worst of times, he could make me laugh. It felt good to sit down even though the ground was cold. I opened my bag and took out more bread, giving a piece to each of the boys. It was stale, but we were so hungry, we hardly noticed.

"How much longer, Mama?" Diet asked.

"Not too much." I replied even though I really had no idea.

"You know what I want, more than anything?" Diet asked.

"To see your father," I replied thinking that's what I wanted more than anything, to be in America with him.

"Yeah, that would be good. I miss him." Gisbert said, hanging his head.

"But more than that I want candy and chicken and my nice warm bed." Diet almost shouted in our faces.

I reached out and hugged him.

"Yes, Diet, we want those things too, but we must keep on. Our next stop is Mannheim."

We stood up and dusted ourselves off, walking on and on. It was late afternoon and we saw more cars and people now. We had to be getting close. A truck pulled over to the side of the road and stopped. The driver rolled down the window and turned his wrinkled face towards us.

"Good day, Frau. Where are you going?"

"Good day!" I replied, hoping he couldn't hear the fear in my voice, "we are on our way to the shoemaker's in Mannheim."

"I am going that way, too. It looks like you could use a ride, especially the boy who needs the shoes," the man said, pointing to Gisbert.

Oh dear! I was caught, didn't know what to say, didn't know if this was a good guy or someone connected to the police. Studying his face, that looked ruddy from too many years in the sun, I fixed my gaze on his dark brown eyes. Then I asked a question to buy some time, to get a better sense of who this man was, friend or enemy.

Being polite I addressed him as Mister, "Herr, do you live in Manheim?"

"Ya! I am the butcher, just coming back from Herr Landmann's. He will have a cow for me tomorrow at noon. I was hoping to get it today, but his help is working on the neighbor's barn." He said as he opened the door.

Diet jumped in before I could say anything more. We had to accept his ride now. I couldn't pull him out without making the driver suspicious. So I helped Gisbert climb up and then got in myself.

"So where are you coming from?" the driver asked.

"Reichenbach," I lied a little using the name of the neighboring town. Fearful that if we were caught, they could track down exactly who we were, if I had told the truth about being from Langenbielau.

"Well, that's a long walk. No wonder you look tired and worn. I'm sure Herr Schuhmacher will let you rest tonight at his place. His Frau is very nice; you'll like her. Does he know you are coming?"

"I don't know. My mother wrote to him, but the post hasn't been very reliable in our town lately."

"Hmm" the butcher replied, stroking his chin.

That worried me. Maybe he was not one to trust. Where was he taking us? Was he really going to Mannheim?

"How much farther to Mannheim?" I asked in the bravest voice I could manage.

"About half an hour."

We rode along in silence for a while, having no way to tell if we were actually on our way to Mannheim or not.

"Do they have candy there?" Diet asked.

I was grateful for him to break the tenseness.

"But of course," the butcher said with a chuckle, "we even have a candy store. So what's your favorite?"

"Chocolate." Diet replied as if the driver would produce a piece instantly, like a magician.

More people and cars on the roads made me feel better. We had to be getting closer to Mannheim. The driver seemed to genuinely like Diet. I wondered if he had children. We passed more side roads and the large farm fields seemed to be behind us.

"Okay, close your eyes, Kleinkind, and when we come around the next turn, you'll see Mannheim," the butcher said to Diet.

The town came into view, and I sighed with relief. A whole street of neat shops, two stories high. The shop owners probably lived above them. On one side of the street was a tall white building, with a balcony on the second story. Just below it, the words "Town Hall" were etched into the white stone. The butcher slowed down and stopped in front of the shop with the blue shutters.

"Well, here you are."

He hopped out, standing a lot taller than I had expected. The butcher came around, opened my door, and offered his hand to help me out. Then he helped Gisbert down, and Diet tumbled out of the truck, laughing and looking for the candy store."

"Vielen Dank (Thank you very much)," I said to the butcher.

He smiled at me and then stared for a few moments. Just as I began to feel uncomfortable, he walked to the other side of the truck, got in and said "I'll stop by tomorrow with some candy for the Klienkind. The candy store is closed for the day."

"Oh please, don't worry about that. We are most grateful for the ride." I cried after him as he drove away.

Then I took the boys' hands and walked over to the front of the shoe store, hoping the skinny boy was right about the shoemaker and his wife. As I knocked on the door, I listened. Nothing. I knocked a little louder. Then I heard

Step…klop…..step……klop...step…..klop.

"Warte mal, (wait a minute)" a small voice called.

As the uneven steps came closer, I looked at our shabby clothes, moistened my finger with spit and pushed Diet's hair out of his face.

"Mama, look at the sign," Gisbert said.

"Alfons Der Schuhmacher" was carved in wood with the outline of a shoe in the background.

"Ya, so we are in the right place," I answered.

"Mama, someone has talent. The lettering is perfect."

The door opened with a creak. A boy about the size of Dietfried stood there.

"Good day! I am sorry we can't keep the door unlocked any

more. The police just came, asked questions, and tried to give us trouble. Most times if they have to wait for someone to open the door, they will go on by. I am Heinrich, this is my father's shop. Come in and he'll be here in a little while."

"Thank you, Heinrich."

As he stepped back to let us in I realized that he had one shoe with a very thick sole. The shiny red-brown color distracted me from watching his uneven gait as he led us to chairs in the front room.

"Mmm. What's that smell?" Diet asked.

"Our shop, our whole house, actually, smells like this. I hardly notice anymore. It's leather." Heinrich answered, "Do you like it?"

"Ya, I guess. How old are you?"

"Diet, please be polite," I said.

"It's okay. I'm fifteen," Heinrich replied.

"Really? How can you be older than Gisbert? He's not even twelve, but you're littler."

A stout woman shuffled into the room, and said "Hi I'm Hildegard. How can we help you? Who needs shoes?"

"Well, Gisbert has been hobbling a lot," I said as my hand motioned toward my older son.

Hildegard looked down at his feet and told him to take off his boots.

"Ach du Himmel! How long have these been on your feet, lad?" she exclaimed.

The leather smell was not strong enough to cover the stench; it was so bad, as if Gisbert's feet had died. I was so ashamed. Maybe this was not a good idea. What if Hildegard figured out that we were running from the police? We couldn't leave then though. That would certainly have raised suspicion.

"Heinrich, go and fetch the foot-bucket, fill it with water and salt," his mother ordered.

She turned to me and the questions began.

"So what are your names? Where are you from? Are you in trouble? Do you have money?"

"We are Ida, Gisbert and Dietfried from Reichenbach. We are going to my sister's house in Hamburg." I was careful to keep my story the same as what I had told the butcher.

"Such a long trip! No wonder you look exhausted! Did you come all the way on foot?" Hildegard asked, staring straight through me.

Was she expecting that we were going to give her trouble? She seemed kind enough to get something for Gisbert's feet.

"Yes, we are very tired. We travelled all the way from Heidelberg today, and only a little while ago, the butcher offered us a ride. Surely it would have been after dark if he hadn't been so kind," I answered trying to make it seem like we knew the butcher, at least a little.

In the back of my mind I thought of the Romas and Joshua, since he was the one who told us about the shoemaker of Mannheim.

It's always best not to say too much, so I didn't mention them.

"Well, I suppose we can offer you some floor space for the night. At least it'll be warmer than outside."

Step….klop…step…..klop, we heard Heinrich coming back. I went over and took his foot-bucket, placed it in front of Gisbert and peeled off his smelly socks with crusted blood on them. His feet were blistered and black and blue. Embarrassed, I pushed them into the bucket so Hildegard didn't see how bad they looked.

She seemed to sense how uncomfortable I felt, and said "It's okay Ida, we've seen everything from gnarled and torn-up feet to ones with bad frost-bite. Let me get my husband, Alfons."

Hildegard went to the back room. A fellow with stooped shoulders came out and trudged toward us barely lifting his feet off the floor. His eyes peered out through bushy blond eyebrows.

Looking straight at Gisbert, he remarked as if to himself "Hmm, what have we here?"

Getting down in front of Gisbert, he lifted one foot out of the water then the other, gently placing them on a towel. As he moved the bucket aside, he looked around for Gisbert's boots.

"Frau, these are too small, and all these cracks made blisters. It will take me a few weeks to make him new shoes and they'll cost five Reichmarks," the shoemaker said in a gentle voice.

"I have no Reichmarks, but I do have some coins to offer you. Will that be okay? We really had hoped to get on our way sooner and we have no place to stay for that long."

"Well, I do have a pair I made for the Ehrlich boy. He and his family just disappeared one night; I doubt they'll be back for the shoes," he said as his voice trailed off sadly.

He walked to a shelf and picked up a pair of shiny black shoes.

"Hilde, do you have an extra pair of socks, heavy ones?" He shouted toward the back room.

"Ya, I will look."

Gisbert dried his feet as Diet slept curled up across two chairs.

Hildegard came shuffling in waving brown socks in one hand and a needle and thread in the other.

"These should do, but the hole in the heel needs mending," she said as she handed everything to me, "Now I must prepare dinner."

"Thank you, so much." I took them and began darning, happy to have something to keep my hands busy.

Alfons went to the window and peeked behind the curtains, he moved to the door, checked the locks, and secured the wooden bar across it.

He turned to Diet, still sleeping on the chairs. His mouth curled up at the ends and he broke into a cheery smile.

"Ah... I remember when Heinrich was smaller than that... only he was so tiny and crippled, they told us he'd never walk. At the hospital, there were many children in wheelchairs and a few on crutches. That's when I decided to be not just an ordinary shoemaker like my father, but one who made shoes for these children so they could walk. I experimented with all kinds of materials for Heinrich's shoes as the nurse and his mother both tried to get his legs strong enough. The doctor helped me design a brace with wood and leather that he wore to bed every night for a few years. That straightened his legs, then I made a shoe with a lift, but it was so heavy, Heinrich couldn't move it. His sister and brother helped him a lot and made him chase them. They always let him catch them when he got tired," Alfons reminisced.

Soon I finished the darning and brought the socks for Gisbert to put on. He rubbed his feet with the warm, thick socks on them and looked up with a great big smile, the first one I had seen on his face since the day of the Hitler Youth Parade.

"That's why God put us on this earth," Alfons said, "now put the shoes on and let's go see if dinner is ready," .

Gisbert carefully took one shoe, trying not to touch the shine, put it over the thick sock and tied it. Then he did the same with the second shoe, moving his hands as if he was a brain surgeon. Then he hopped up and danced a funny jig. I laughed. He did this funny 'German jig' all the way to the back room. Diet rubbed his eyes and wanted to know what we were doing there. He got off the chair and asked if he was getting new shoes too. Telling him 'not today' made me sad again. I tried not to show it since Alfons was watching me.

#

When we went to the back room, there was a little girl who

washed her hands and set bowls on the large wooden table. She asked her mother if eight was right and Hildegard nodded. A tall boy came lumbering down the stairs, went to the sink, washed his hands and then sat down. Alfons took the armchair at the head of the table and introduced us to Heidemarie and Bertram. Hildegard ladled soup with leeks, potatoes and onions into each bowl, as everyone else sat down. Then she placed a loaf of bread on the table and joined us. Alfons said a prayer as we all bowed our heads. I was so grateful for this one short piece of normal life.

Chapter Thirteen

On the Way to Hamburg 1934

We slept on the floor in the back room with the large wooden
table. It was still very early when Hildegard told us that we had to
leave as soon as we could this morning. I had washed our clothes and
hung them by the fire for the night; what a treat it was to have clean
clothes again!

Alfons came down and we sat at the table to barter my coins
for the shoes, socks and Reichmarks to get passage on the train to
Hamburg. Counting out my coins, I decided to part with half of them,
hoping that would leave us enough to get to my sister's. Alfons went
to a cabinet, opened a safe and took out a wad of bills. Money
seemed to be worth less every day. We tried to figure out the price of
the train fare to be sure we had enough for that, a little something for
bread and whatever else might come. Alfons took coins for the shoes
and exchanged more for Reichmarks so I'd be able to buy our tickets.
Hildegard was busy making sure I paid him for Giesbert's shoes as
well. Alfons and I were both happy with the transaction. So Alfons
told Hildegard it was over, and asked her to please make some coffee
and porridge.

I woke the boys up, and got them dressed. Diet couldn't find his shoes. Just as we started to look for them, I heard the klop...step...klop...step... of Heinrich coming in from the other room. He held out a pair of shiny shoes to Diet, who grabbed them up and started to dance around. I was afraid that I didn't have enough money to pay for these too.

Heinrich said "These were Bertram's old, old shoes that I hid when I was little because someday I thought I'd wear normal shoes like him. I just polished them last night and I want Diet to have them. Papa said it was okay to give them to him and they should fit."

Diet put on the shoes, jumped up and down, and moved his arms in every direction. What a little clown! We laughed. When he finally settled down, he went over and hugged Heinrich.

Food was the only thing that would distract them. We ate our porridge with dried berries and thanked Hildegard and Alfons. Diet wanted to stay and play with Heinrich and Heidemarie. Alfons gave him two scraps of leather as a going away present, and Diet finally agreed to gather up his things. Alfons gave us directions to the train station, and ushered us out the back door.

We walked toward the train station, the boys close behind me. It was important that we acted as normal as possible and didn't attract attention. Trying to be aware of everyone and everything around me, we hurried along, since I wasn't sure when the train to Hamburg came. If we missed it, we could be stuck in Manheim for another day with no place to go.

We heard the whistle blow just as we got there. I grabbed the boys' hands and we ran to the window, my skirt and scarf flying. Only six people were in front of us in line, but they moved as slowly as inchworms on a twig.

"A train ride! A train ride! We are going on a train!" Diet shouted as he jumped up and down.

"Shh! You will be going nowhere unless you are quiet and wait in line like a good boy," I commanded as I grabbed his arm.

My admonition was too late. A police officer was heading in our direction. My hands tightened on my bag and I felt a lump form in my throat.

The shiny black boots stomped over to the line, my heart stopped. The policeman started asking each person behind us where they were going and why. I looked up at the window, only two people in front of us. Please hurry, I thought. Then one. The policeman was talking to the person behind us as I stepped up to the window, and exchanged the Reichmarks for our tickets.

"Not so fast, Frau!" a commanding voice came from behind me.

I froze.

"Where are you going?" he demanded.

"To Hamburg." I replied, thinking there was something familiar about this man.

"Why?" his sharp voice cut into me.

"To see my sister. She is ill and I beg you to let us go now so we don't miss this train."

"Ach! Ya," he said as he stepped aside to let us pass. It was then that I noticed the ugly red birthmark on the side of his face. I couldn't get on the train fast enough, hoping he didn't recognize us from the day he marched into our house wanting to know why the boys weren't at the Hitler youth parade. No time to think about that. I ran with the boys to the train and made sure it was the one to Hamburg.

We got on and I pushed the boys into the first empty seats.

"What was that all about?" Gisbert asked, "Wasn't he the one who came to the house?"

"Shh! Just sit and be quiet until this train is moving," I snapped at him, impatiently.

The conductor came and checked our tickets.

The train was full and I looked around at all the passengers. Many of them looked scruffy like us, and a few were in nice clothes.

"TwooHoo!" the whistle blew and we were on our way. Diet and Gisbert fought over who sat by the window. I made them take turns and watched from the middle as farmlands and little villages zoomed past.

Chapter Fourteen

Oklahoma City 1956

"Ach du Liebe! It's very late. I got caught up in the story and your grandfather will be home any minute. Get into your PJs and brush your teeth as fast as little jackrabbits!" Grandma gently pushed us toward the bathroom.

Grandma was right; in no time at all we heard the car on the gravel driveway.

"Shh! Pretend you are asleep," Annie whispered.

#

When I woke up the sun made me cover my eyes, and I barely opened them.

"What a sleepyhead," Grandpa said. He ruffled my hair with his hand, which was big enough to cover my whole face.

"Do you feel okay? You must have done something very tiring yesterday."

I opened my mouth and start to say "Grandma..."

Annie butted in "took us for a really long walk in the afternoon and we read story books after dark."

Annie gave me a look and I knew why she lied, so I didn't say anything more that might get Grandma in trouble. I hopped out of bed and went to the bathroom.

We spent the day watching cartoons, playing in the yard, and helping Grandma make dumplings. The day went by fast, probably 'cause I got up so late.

As soon as Grandpa left for work, Grandma set the alarm clock.

"There, now when that goes off, it'll be bedtime."

Then she told us about Hamburg.

Chapter Fifteen

Hamburg 1934-36

The train stopped again and again. Each time Diet asked if this was Hamburg. When the train stopped in Hannover it was almost dark. Police got on and walked through the cars. I pretended that I was sleeping, but watched them gruffly pull a woman with black curly hair out of her seat in front of me.

"Go stand at the door, now!" the policeman commanded. The officer left her and turned back toward us.

My scarf covered my head, but he stared at Diet, then reached down and brushed his hand through Diet's blond hair. I wanted to grab his hand and shout at him not to touch my son. Instead I stayed perfectly still. After a minute, he moved on. I sighed with relief. The shiny black boots took deliberate steps forward. His arms moved fast as lightening, two more passengers were yanked to their feet and shoved out the door. I held my breath. Then the officer got off and soon the train was moving again.

I hoped we were getting close to Hamburg. We were all very hungry. I reached into my bag and found part of a loaf of bread. It was hard to break without making lots of crumbs. I did the best I could to share it with the hungry boys trying not to let anyone else see that we were eating. The bread was so stale it barely had any taste.

We kept riding on the train into the night. The boys were restless and I was trying to figure out what to do next. We might have to stay at the station until daylight, since I had no idea how to get to Minne's from there. I dozed off and woke up many times through the night; the boys alternately slept and squabbled.

#

Finally we pulled into the station in Hamburg. It was almost morning, and I was hungry and exhausted. I woke the boys and we got off the train. In the station, a man was sweeping the floors and I asked him how to get to Neumeyerstrasse. He sent us down Abcstrasse to HoheBleichen, then onto Wexstrasse, Grossneumarkt and Steinweg over Millentordamm to Neumayerstrasse. I cleared my head and memorized all the directions, hoping he was telling us correctly. We walked along, glad to be off the train. The streets were crowded with people and the smell of fish was in the air. One street after another, I knew we were getting closer. As we turned onto Neumayerstrasse, there was the Bäkerie sign and the Zigarregeschäft next to it. We were there at last! The wonderful smell of yeast bread consumed us as we opened the door. I went to the lady behind the counter.

"Ach du Himmel! Is that you, Ida?" Minne asked with excitement as she threw her arms around me, "and the Kinder! How they have grown! It's wonderful to see you, but how did you come here and why? The last letters I got from mother, she said you just disappeared and no one knew your whereabouts. She was in your house, found the note and couldn't make sense of it. So she took all of the valuable things out, including the wine glasses from your wedding day, and has kept them in her basement, hoping you'd come back. We feared for the worst." Minne spoke as she hugged Diet and Gisbert.

"You look so thin and tired. You must be starving! You and the boys take anything here in the bakery and come on into our living space in the back. I can't wait to tell Robert you are here!"

The boys grabbed Kuchen and I cut a large slice of bread. Customers came in, so I sent the boys to the back and told the customers that the owner would be back in a minute. When Minne came in, she called each customer by name and packaged their favorite breads, rolls and pastries. Robert rushed over and hugged me as he guided me to the back room out of earshot of the others in the bakery.

"We thought you had fallen into trouble, what with your husband long gone to America. No one had heard from you in such a long time. You must tell us the whole story over dinner," Robert said, shaking his head in disbelief.

The boys were running around and exploring every corner of the back of the store.

"Minne will close a little early today and fix us all a nice supper. You rest and the boys can play with my chess set here. I'd better get back to my Zigarre (Cigar) store," Robert said as he slipped out the back door.

Dinner was incredible! Minne pulled out her finest dishes and had two kinds of wurst with potatoes, string beans, squash and sauerkraut. We even had butter on our bread! It felt like a holiday, and we were treated like royalty!

#

We settled into a routine, helping Minne and Robert in their stores. They made a small space for us with bunk beds for the boys and a cot for me behind the storage room. It was cozy and we felt safe. Gisbert made deliveries all over town for his Tante Minne and Onkel Robert. Diet found a friend at the hatmaker's store after being in Hamburg a few weeks. Since summer was almost over, and we didn't know how much longer we'd be here, we decided it best to enroll the boys in school, which we did.

When I took our papers to the town hall, I realized our family had been apart four long years already. I hoped and prayed that they had no way to trace the incident in Langenbielau to us. It was far enough away and chances were slim. So here we had to act as if we belonged and were just waiting to go join my husband in America. The months passed and I wondered if we'd ever see him again. We had no address for him and he didn't know we were in Hamburg.

#

One day Gisbert came running into the store after a delivery. I was in the kitchen taking bread out of the oven.

"Tante Minne! Tante Minne! Guess What?! I took the pastries to the museum and on my way back I found this huge patch of four leaf clovers in Elbpark!" Gisbert was so excited.

"Wonderful! Gisbert, you will be so lucky! So did you bring me one?" Tante Minne asked.

"There were so many I didn't know which one to pick, but I'll go back now and get some for everyone," he said, as he pulled the money for the pastries out of his pocket and handed it to Minne.

Gisbert disappeared into the street and headed back to the park. Hours passed. It was almost dark when he returned, hanging his head.

"Tante Minne, I am so sorry, I just couldn't find them again, not a one, not a single four-leaf clover. I looked and looked, tried to retrace my steps, but couldn't find a one. At 13, I should be old enough to know better than to leave a whole patch of four-leaf clovers without picking one."

"It's all right. Your luck is our luck." Minne said and she hugged Gisbert.

Chapter Sixteen

Oklahoma 1956

"Grandma, were the four leaf clovers really lucky?" Annie asked.

"You'll find out tomorrow. Time for bed now."

We whispered in bed trying to figure out what lucky thing happened to Gisbert.

"Do you think he finds a leprechaun with a pot of gold in the park?" I asked.

"I think they are only in fairytales, or if they're real, they live in Ireland not Germany." Annie answered.

"Maybe Gisbert got a new friend, or a baby cousin."

"The cousin would be lucky for Tante Minne and Onkel Robert, too."

"What about a candy store?"

"Shh, now girls, it's time to go to sleep. You'll find out tomorrow," Grandma said in a hushed tone, as she tucked us in and kissed us each good night.

Chapter Seventeen

Hamburg 1936

A few days after Gisbert found the four leaf clovers, the postman brought a letter addressed to me. When I opened it, my hands were shaking; it was from the town hall. The letter said to come down and get your passport. We were going to America after all! I shouted to Minne and Robert that we got a letter! It was so exciting! I got the boys as we all needed to have our pictures taken. We put on our best clothes and went right away. Diet hopped on one foot, then the other.

"Come, come!" I tried to hurry the boys along.

"Mama, Where are we going? Why are we in such a hurry?" Gisbert had never seen me this excited.

"We are going to get our passport to America!"

"Where's that?" Diet asked.

"Far away where your Daddy is." I said hoping to get them to move along.

"You mean far away like the shoemaker's house? We need to go there and get me some new shoes; these are too small. Besides I want to play with Heidemarie and Heinrich."

"Diet, we are going far, far away, to America. We'll take a big boat across the ocean." I said trying to convince him that he really wanted to go. But he stopped, and pulled back on my hand.

"I don't want to go. I want new shoes and I want to stay here." Diet pouted.

"You will get new shoes in America and lots more."

"But I want them now!"

"Diet, come. No passport. No new shoes, I said firmly."

He started to follow me again.

"Mama, what about Tante Minne and Onkel Robert? Will we have to leave them? And the wonderful bakery?" Gisbert asked.

"I guess we will, for now. But they might get their papers and follow us soon," I said, hoping it was true.

We got to the huge building and found the hallway to where the letter told us to go. The line was very long and we had to wait and wait. Diet was jumping up and down. He got free of my hand and ran down the hallway. A police officer stepped out of a doorway. Diet froze as he looked down at the shiny black boots."

"And just who do you belong to?" a firm, deep voice asked.

Diet came running to me and hid behind my skirt. He was quiet the rest of the long wait. I was nervous as the officer paced the hallway with a rhythmic klump…klump... klump…klump…I could only think of the sound of the boots on my front steps that day in Langenbielau before we left. I didn't think I'd ever see my little house or my mother and father again. Sadness began to creep over me, I had to think only about going to America and being with my husband. My boys would have a father again. When I got to the front of the line, they took our pictures, I signed papers, and paid them the Reichsmarks.

"Next week on Friday, your passport will be ready. Come to the table in the back hallway and present this card," the young lady said.

"Next," she looked to the person behind me.

As the sun shone over the city, we made our way to the ships in the harbor and looked at the huge ocean liners. The boys were getting excited about going too. I told them we had to wait a week for the passport. But we could go and check the fares and the dates when the ships would be leaving. The next passage was on October 6; the cost was high, but with the remaining coins from home and help from Minne and Robert, we'd be able to go. We needed to be sure to have our passport first; you never knew when things could change, especially in this crazy time. I was afraid our luck might run out.

#

All week Minne, Robert and I sat up late talking about everything we remembered from when we were small, and what we hoped for. Too bad our mother was so far away in Neurode. Emil, our youngest brother, was still close by her, and that was some comfort.

When Friday finally came, I left the boys at the bakery and went down to the town hall alone, knowing I would have no patience with Diet, and if he misbehaved and called attention to us, they might not give me the ReisePass as promised. The line was much shorter and when I got to the hall table a lady in a black suit asked my name and rifled through dark green booklets in the box.

"Ah, this is it," she said flipping open the page and looking at my picture attached with two little round metal circles.

"Occupation?"

"Housekeeper," I answered.

"Birthplace?" she asked.

"Langenbielau"

"Date of birth?"

"14th May 1901."

"Residence?"

"Altona"

Then she looked at me and wrote Oval face, Gray-blue eyes, blond hair. She asked the boys' names and birth-dates and entered these on the page as well. She handed me the pen to sign my name. My hand was shaking; I took a deep breath and steadied my hand, hoping it would be readable. She examined my signature and looked at my picture again.

"After this is official you will get a letter to go to the American Consulate. They will give you a Quota Immigration Visa number in about a month."

She folded the booklet and handed it to the police officer standing tall and straight like a light pole. He stamped it and signed it. Then he thrust it at me with a disgusted look.

"Danke," I mumbled as I clutched the precious booklet and turned to leave.

As soon as I was down the long hallway, I stopped and looked at the passport. An eagle on the cover was standing atop a wreath with a swastika in the center. I tried hard not to show how I felt about this one more proof that the Nazis were taking over. I was so afraid for my country.

#

The days passed and I worried about everything, uncertainty was my only emotion. On the one hand I was anxious to get to America and to be with my husband. On the other hand I had no idea how I'd find him, what we'd do there, where we'd live, or how I'd manage to learn English. So many things weighed on my mind. I would miss Minne, Robert and the bakery so much. They had been very kind to take us in and take care of us. But I knew we could not stay and continue to be a burden on them.

On the second day of November, a letter came from the American Consulate. We had been assigned Quota numbers 4135, 4136 and 4137. I counted out the money and carefully tucked it in my bag. Then I went to the dockyard and purchased our tickets. Thank goodness we were leaving, while I still had enough money. The prices kept going up for everything; it was terrible. Next I went to the Consulate, hoping I didn't have to pay them. The line was long and I was happy not to have Diet with me. When I stepped up and handed the man my passport and the letter, he opened it and shook his head.

"Is something wrong?" I asked.

"I need to see the two children to stamp and approve this. You will have to bring them back with you."

"I can do that tomorrow, but can you tell me what the cost will be?" I asked nervously.

"There is no charge. I will see the three of you tomorrow then, okay?"

I left hanging my head and holding the passport tightly all the way back to Minne's.

"What's the matter?" Minne asked as soon as I walked into the bakery.

"I don't have the consulate stamps yet. I must bring the boys with me."

"Not to worry, you can do that tomorrow. We will miss you so, but it's a lucky thing you are leaving for America. We are happy for you to be able to make a new life there." Minne said as she hugged me, covering my coat and skirt with flour. We both laughed and dusted ourselves off.

The next day I returned to the consulate with the boys. Diet promised to be good if I took him back to see the big ships. We got our stamps and numbers. The gentleman at the consul gave us his official signature. Then we stopped at the harbor and checked on the dates and times that the ship was leaving for America, November 6 at 9:30 in the morning. When we got back I told Minne that we'd be leaving in two days and we washed clothes so we could pack the next day. We didn't have much so it didn't take long.

Chapter Eighteen

Oklahoma City 1956

"Grandma, you are almost to America, now aren't you?" I asked.

"Yes, Liebling, and it's a good thing because Grandpa and I will be driving you home to Virginia in two days. I'll wash our clothes and hang them to dry tomorrow."

"Just like you did when you came to America," Annie said, "but we don't have to buy tickets for a boat, 'cause we'll just pile in the car."

"Yes, girls, it's going to be a long trip too. We'll be driving for three days and three nights," Grandma warned us.

Later in the day, Grandpa left to run errands and we picked all the vegetables in the garden.

Chapter Nineteen

To America 1936

The day had finally arrived. Minne and Robert came with us
to the harbor and helped carry our bags. We hugged them good-by
with tears in our eyes; my throat was so choked up, no words came
out. We finally let go of each other, Minne and Robert turned back.
He put his arm around her shoulder as she held her Taschentuch
(handkerchief) to her face. We walked up the long ramp with a crowd
of other people.

When we got to the top, two policemen were standing there,
making everyone get into a single line. One checked our passport,
looking first at our pictures, then at us. The other one handed printed
fliers to the boys. Gisbert looked at them and then at me, when the
tall policeman told him that he needed to join the Nazi party in
America. This was the information on how he was to do it.

*Oh no! Don't say anything Gisbert, I thought. He might kick
us off the ship.* I nodded my head and told him to take the papers.
Diet looked at me and scrunched up his face. I watched the policeman
and hoped he hadn't seen Diet's expression.

"Yes, Dietfreid, this is important, take it," I said as we were being pushed forward.

He took the fliers as I caught my breath; we tried to move along the railing so we could wave to Minne and Robert. I was careful to put the passport in a safe place in my bag. People were pushing and shoving and there were so many of us on this ship, it no longer seemed so big. We heard shouts and men were running and pulling ropes. The Polizei went back down the ramp and the ship pulled away from the dock.

It wasn't long before the land was behind us. I brought the boys inside and we took seats. It was cloudy and windy and we were tossed about by the rough waves. The ship was listing from one side to the other. Gisbert told me that his stomach felt queasy and we went back out on the deck; a good thing, as we no sooner got there and he started throwing up over the side. Then Diet did the same. We held on to the railing and our bags for what seemed like hours. Finally, the seas calmed and we were okay.

The next night we saw the moon over the ocean and we went back up on the deck. I took out the papers the Nazi police officer gave us. Diet and Gisbert were looking at me, with no idea of what to expect. It was our private little ceremony. I tossed all the fliers overboard into the middle of the Atlantic Ocean. We would be far away from Hitler and his Nazi followers for the rest of our lives. Whatever America would be like, I knew it would be a better life for us than staying in Germany with the leader who was so hungry for power that he would stop at nothing.

We were on the ship for days. Then one sunny morning our clothes were blowing as we stood on the deck.

Gisbert pointed, "Look! Look! That's land there, isn't it?"

"Who is that big tall green lady?" Diet asked.

"It's the Statue of Liberty, welcoming us to New York," a voice from behind us announced.

Then shouts erupted all over the ship. "America!" "New York!" "We made it!" "Gott sei Dank!" "God be thanked."

PART II

A SNEEZE IN THE ATTIC

Chapter Twenty

Madison Wisconsin 1981

Do you ever get the feeling that you've been somewhere before, the French refer to it as *déjà vu*? This is how I felt in Madison. Maybe it was the large number of German descendants. They even served brats (German sausages) and beer at the University's student center. So I wasn't surprised to meet a co-worker, Heidi, with a very thick German accent. There was an instant connection, and I knew we'd become very good friends.

As it turned out, Heidi lived two houses down the street from me. She invited me over for coffee one day after work. I was delighted to have a chance to practice my rusty German and to get to know her. After parking my car in the garage, I walked over to Heidi and Jack's house and rang the doorbell. She welcomed me into her tidy living room and hung up my coat.

"Let's sit at the kitchen table," Heidi said as she motioned to the doorway where the aroma of fresh coffee drifted into the rest of the house. The room was cozy with a large, round table in the center. Heidi was setting beautifully painted coffee cups on the ironed mauve tablecloth. On the walls hung wooden and decorative ceramic plates, symmetrically arranged. One plate caught my eye, not just because it was blue, but it had a picture of a town on it. When I squinted, I thought it said Mannheim.

As Heidi poured our coffee, she smiled and said, "the instant I saw you, I liked you. I believe in intuition you know, ever since the day my father came home from the war."

Then she looked at me haltingly, as if she thought that might have been the wrong thing to say right away to someone you've only worked with for a few days.

Quickly I replied to reassure her. "You must mean returning from World War II. I'd love to hear the story; you know I believe in something that connects us beyond our current circumstances, too. I guess you could call it intuition, but I kind of think it's something more. Please, go on with your story."

She sliced the warm cake she just took out of the oven.

"Heidi, you are going to spoil my dinner with that, you know," I said jokingly, "how did you ever have time to make it after work?"

"I love this pound cake, and so I bake a few at a time and freeze them. I only had to heat it up this afternoon."

"Mmm… it smells just like my grandmother's."

As soon as Heidi sat down, I urged her to get on with her story.

Chapter Twenty-One

Mannheim 1937

Heidi's story begins…

In our town, on the main street, were many shops, and all the owners lived upstairs. Life was good before the war. We had plenty, and my mother said it was because of my brother, Heinrich. You see he was born with crooked feet and legs and doctors said he'd never walk. My father was from a family of shoemakers, and he decided to make special shoes for Heinrich. With the shoes, a leg brace my father designed, and the patience of my mother, he learned to walk. The doctors were amazed and word spread all over Germany. We had important people bring their children to my father's humble shop and they paid him well. Things had started to change when the Nazi party took over. All over Germany, we were supposed to boycott Jewish-owned businesses. The people of Mannheim pretty much ignored that, since these people had been our neighbors and friends for as long as we could remember.

One day Der Führer, Hitler, came to Mannheim. That was the beginning of the end. He thought he was too important to stand on the same ground as the rest of us. So he gave a speech from the second floor of the town hall. Of course everybody had to come.

We listened to him shout about how he was going to make Germany, Der Vaterland, the best country in the world, how he would get rid of the shame of defeat from the world war. On and on he ranted, and blamed the Jews for all the economic problems. When the townspeople had had enough, someone pushed him off the balcony. Hitler's mouth opened wide, and we expected a blood-curdling scream to come out. His expression turned to rage and indignation as he landed in the bushes. His face was scratched, but he was not dead, as we should have hoped.

A police officer, a young, handsome fellow, reached out and helped him to his feet. As soon as he was standing, the officer thrust his arm out straight with a "Heil Hitler", and rushed the speaker over to the black Mercedes.

Hitler's face was still red with anger and his brow furrowed. He held a clenched fist up to the crowd and shouted, "Mannheim will pay for this! No one embarrasses Der Führer!"

As the SS officer got into the car, I noticed a strange red mark on the side of his face, just above his eye. Everyone came rushing out of the building in a frenzy. The other police came racing out into the street. It was bedlam.

That incident is embedded in my memory, as if it happened yesterday. I can still see them getting into the cars, the shiny black boots were the last image before doors slammed shut. The cars sped away with swastika flags waving, reminding us that this was Nazi power. When the cars were out of sight, a calm, a foreboding silence filled the streets. So many people and not a sound, not even a whisper.

Chapter Twenty-Two

Madison Wisconsin 1981

"Oh my, Heidi! This is incredible! All these years I thought my grandmother was the only one who hated Hitler. She always said that he was hungry for power and would stop at nothing."

"Oh, the whole town saw right through him. Mannheim was hit with inflation, but not as bad as most of Germany. I was only a kid then, but the adults talked and I listened, even when I wasn't supposed to," Heidi said with a bit of a grin.

"Wait at minute! You were the shoemaker's daughter in Mannheim in the 1930's! My grandmother told us of this kind family who gave my father a pair of shoes and helped them get to Hamburg. That must have been your family. As I remember, Grandma said they had three children, two boys and a girl. Her name was Heidemarie."

"Ach du Himmel! That's me! I just go by Heidi here, but that's my real name. We were the only shoemakers in Mannheim. So what you are saying means that your Grandma knew my family. Is that right?" Heidi said in disbelief.

"Well, she, my Dad and my uncle left Langenbielau, and hid from the Nazi soldiers with gypsies in the forest until they could make their way to Heidelberg and Mannheim. From there, they went on to Hamburg, and stayed with Grandma's sister until they got passage to America in 1936. They stayed at the shoemaker's house for only a day, but who knows if they ever would have made it to Hamburg or America if it hadn't been for the kindness of your parents." I explained.

"Hmm…1936, I was eight years old. I could have been that little girl your Grandma talked about. Did she say anything about my brother Heinrich?" Heidi asked.

"Just as you described him, and she spoke of your older brother, Bertram, wasn't it?"

"Yes! Your Grandmother *must* have been at our house all those years ago!" Heidi exclaimed.

"They say it's a small world, but not just in places and people we know, but in time as well. Coincidences?...I wonder," my thoughts spilled out of my mouth as quickly as they came into my mind.

Heidi glanced at the clock and interrupted.

"Oh, dear! It's almost six and time for Jack to come home. I'll put soup on the stove to warm up, and get out the fresh bread."

"Yes, I'd better get going. I still have some lab data to look at tonight and that presentation for corporate to finish. Thank you so much for the coffee, cake and most of all for the good conversation. I can't wait until we can get together again to hear more of the story."

"How about Thursday after work?" Heidi asked.

"Sure, I'll see you then."

Chapter Twenty-Three

Mannheim 1938-39

Thursday after work - Heidi's story continues...

Things got pretty bad for our Jewish friends. Their German citizenship was taken away and the police put up signs everywhere that said '*No Jews Allowed*'. The authorities caught up with my father and my older brother; they were informed of a mandatory military draft. Daddy worked night and day to use all his leather to make ordinary shoes. That way he thought mother would be able to sell them when he was gone, and at least we'd have some income.

Mother stayed up with him and I heard them talking about how badly the government was treating our Jewish neighbors. Their children were no longer in school with us. It became almost impossible for Jews to get passports to travel outside Germany. I didn't tell them that my teacher was fired. When the new person came to take over our class, she said that he refused to teach the truth that Jews and Non-Aryans were racially inferior. I didn't believe it, but I was smart enough not to say so.

There were also the times when our Jewish neighbors would

just disappear in the night, never to be seen or heard from again.

Then Kristallnacht happened. It was all over the news. Synagogues were burned. Jewish stores, homes and schools were no longer safe. Then the Nazis blamed the Jews for the looting and destruction, making them pay fines for the damages. How terribly unfair that was!

Soon the awful day came when father and Bertram had to leave. We hugged and cried. Father told us to be very careful and to hide Heinrich because there was probably some truth to the rumors that the Nazis were putting to death anyone with a disability. Mother cried harder and I told her I'd be with her. Her brother and his wife lived out in the country, a three-hour walk from Mannheim. We all agreed that if anything happened, and we couldn't stay in our house, that's where we'd go. We all cried and hugged some more, then we watched them leave town with the other men. We didn't go back inside until they were completely out of sight. Mama muttered something about hoping and praying they wouldn't get swallowed up in this Nazi nonsense. Then she covered her mouth and looked all around us. I thought that no one else heard her, but I wasn't sure.

Chapter Twenty-Four

Mannheim 1940

We managed all right, for a while. Mother sold a pair of shoes here and there. We kept Heinrich out of the store, and I made up games and puzzles out of cardboard for him to do so he would stay upstairs. I studied and read to him when I wasn't in school or helping mother. We brought his food up to him and I cleaned his dishes. It wasn't like life with father and Bertram, but mother said we had no choice but to make do.

Things got worse. Hitler invaded Poland, and Germany was at war. Mother worried and prayed all the time. It had been awhile since she'd sold any shoes, and I wondered if we were running out of money.

One night, we heard awful noises, screeching in the sky. Mother ran into our room and scooped up Heinrich.

"Quick! Quick! Downstairs! Now!"

We rushed to the back of the store and mother opened the door to the cellar and pushed me down the stairs. She mustered some superhuman strength that night carrying Heinrich down all those stairs.

"Boom! Crash!" the noise was deafening. It seemed as if the whole world was tumbling down. We huddled together in the cellar for what seemed like hours.

#

Finally, everything was quiet. Heinrich had fallen asleep in Mama's lap. I was anxious to see what had happened. Mother insisted we wait awhile longer as she was sure it was still dark. This wasn't a time to argue, so I just slowly crept up the steps. When I got to the top I tried to push the door open. It wouldn't budge.

"Mama, we are trapped! We can't get out!"

At that moment I was sure we were going to die in the cellar.

Mother's voice was calm, "Heidimarie, we will get out and go to Onkel Hansi's in the country."

She carefully took off her robe and laid Heinrich on it. Mama came up the stairs, and leaned her shoulder against the door. She instructed me to push as hard as I could when she counted to three. We pushed and the door moved a few centimeters. We did this again and again until I could squeeze through. There was dust, wood, rocks and bricks everywhere. When I looked up I could see the stars in the sky. Our house was totally destroyed by the bomb. I wanted my best friend Gertrut. As I was ready to make my way to her house, my mother's sharp voice broke the silence.

"Heidemarie, look around and see if you can find any food or clothes in all these heaps. I'll go back and get Heinrich. We need to leave right away!" Mama shouted over her shoulder as she hurried down the stairs.

I stumbled around in the dark in the rubble, thinking our coats should have been hanging by the back door, which had come off its hinges. Mother came up the stairs with Heinrich.

"Oh dear, we really need shoes, especially for Heinrich. How will he ever make it the six kilometers to Neuhofen without them?"

We looked for them in the dark; usually we kept them by the back door. I went over groveling in the dust like a dog, searching for a bone buried long ago. Ah! A piece of wool, I pulled on it, trying to make out the color in the faint light from the moon and stars. Coughing, but happy, I announced that I found a coat, and soon the other two. Then I dug and dug, coming up with broken chunks of our house. Finally I found a shoe, and then another. This was hard work, trying to unearth them, but I finally had all six.

Heinrich was crying. At least we weren't hurt. We shook out our coats and put them on, and then our shoes, but we left everything else behind in the dark. We trudged along through what was left of the streets, being ever so careful not to trip. In the faint moonlight, our eyes adjusted to the shadows. We tiptoed along in a very strange, deserted world. *This must be what it's like on the moon*, I thought to myself. It took a long time just to get out of Mannheim. When the sun started to come up we just kept walking. Heinrich kept asking how much longer, and I felt so sorry for him knowing that as much as my legs hurt, his must have been so much worse. I knew mother was worried that if there were police around, they might see him hobbling and take him away.

We walked over the bridge and kept on going, one step in front of the other, again and again. By daylight we were glad to be out of the city. Heinrich moaned that he was tired and hungry and thirsty. So was I. But we had nothing. Mother promised him we'd be okay when we got to Tante Berta and Onkel Hansi's. We just had to keep going. She picked him up and tried to carry him a little here and there. It seemed like Onkel Hansi's was a thousand kilometers away.

When the sun was overhead, I thought we should have been there already. It used to take us just a few hours to get to their farmhouse. We had been walking all morning. Each time a car or truck passed, mother held Heinrich close and practically froze. My stomach growled and I felt weak. But knowing how much harder it must have been for Heinrich, I didn't dare complain. As we went by a long stand of trees and around the bend, I thought we might be getting close, but I didn't want to get my hopes up.

"We are almost there!" Mama exclaimed.

My whole body wanted to jump for happiness and relief. I saw their house, and started to run. To this day I wonder where I found the energy. I banged on the door with both my little fists. By the time mother and Heinrich got there, Tante Berta had opened the door, her eyes wide and her mouth frozen open.

"Ach! Heidemarie! Hildegard! What's the matter?" she exclaimed as she hugged my mother and then Heinrich and me.

"We've been bombed! I heard them, the planes! We got to the cellar just in time. There's nothing left of our house or the shoe store," Mama said as she burst into tears and then kept sobbing.

Tante Berta put her arms around Mama and held her tight. "You poor dears. You will stay here. Has Bertram gone to the army too?"

"Ya, fourteen is old enough the government thinks."

"You must be starved. I have only a few eggs, as my chickens are getting old. They don't lay much anymore. We had to sell the cows and goats, but we still have vegetables," Tante Berta said as she let go of Mama and went over and lit the stove. She cooked the eggs with potatoes and onions, and set plates on the table. She took out part of a loaf of bread and sliced it for us.

"Sorry, I have no butter for your bread," she apologized.

"We are grateful for anything you can give us, please don't feel badly. Times are hard and you are doing what you can. Danke," my mother reassured her.

We wolfed down our food. It tasted so good and Heinrich and I each drank two glasses of water. Then mother went to the living room, collapsed onto the couch, and fell fast asleep. Heinrich and I were tired too, but I helped Tante Berta clear the table and wash the dishes. I curled up on the rug on the floor and didn't wake up until the next morning.

It wasn't long before Onkel Hansi had to go away to fight in the war. I remembered Daddy and Bertram leaving us and I cried myself to sleep that night.

Why do countries have to fight? Good men go off and many of them die, why? It made no sense to me then and it makes no sense now. Well, the war dragged on. We were hungry all the time, even though we worked very hard. Little brown beetles ate almost all the potatoes we planted. The onions, tomatoes, kohlrabi, kale and beets grew. We ate soup day after day, made from these vegetables. In early winter the kale died, we had run out of kohlrabi and every now and then someone would come and give us a Reichmark for some vegetables. Tante Berta used it to buy flour and saved it. Once she even bought a loaf of bread in town. Now, that was a treat! She made bread, but without butter, it wasn't as good as what Mama used to make.

We got skinny, but we were grateful just to be alive and have something. Every day we prayed for father, Bertram and Hansi. It made me feel like a grownup, working all day, no school, no friends. I missed Gertrut most of all. It was really terrible not even knowing if she was still alive.

Chapter Twenty-Five

Madison 1981

The front door flew open. Heidi and I both jumped and then
froze.

"Anybody home?" Jack asked as he poked his head into the
kitchen.

"Oh my, I didn't realize it was so late," Heidi said as she got
up and gave Jack a hug and a kiss.

"I'm not interrupting anything now, am I? Are you still telling
war stories?" Jack wanted to know. "Don't you ever tire of all that
old stuff?"

"Oh, Jack. Some people find it comforting to talk about it and
others of us just want to try and understand the craziness of
governments and rulers," I said, coming to Heidi's defense.

"It's all very simple, **power**. It goes to their heads. Too bad,
'cause us normal people pay the price. But that's how it is. Okay,
back to the here and now. I'm hungry," Jack said, putting his hand on
his stomach.

Jack looked at us, knowing we hadn't even thought about
food.

"Jack, I think we ought to go out for dinner. It's been a really busy week and tomorrow's Friday. So that's something to celebrate. I'll pay half, what do you say?" I proposed in a slightly pleading tone.

"Sure, if we can go to Perkins." Jack agreed. So Heidi and I got our coats and we piled into Jack's car. On the way he told us the one rule was that our dinner conversation had to be about the present day. We enjoyed dinner and talked about Jack's work and the good people in the lab. Before Jack dropped me off at my house, Heidi and I agreed to meet on Monday after work.

Chapter Twenty-Six

Mannheim 1944

The war went on. One cold, sunny afternoon, cars and trucks came up the road. They stopped at the farm next to ours. I watched out the window as the German soldiers piled out of the vehicles. Mama darted around the house looking for Heinrich. She pulled him away from the bedroom window, and told me to get him up to the attic quickly. She told us that we had to stay there and not make a sound, to listen until we were sure the soldiers were gone, and either Mama or Tante let us know all was clear. I wondered how mother knew they were coming to Tante Berta's.

Heinrich had a hard time climbing the ladder, which was really a bunch of flat boards about four inches deep and a foot wide, nailed to the wall. I kept encouraging him and finally he got to the top and pushed the board out of the way. As he crawled in, I felt a blast of cold air, and rushed to grab a blanket. Then I climbed up the steps as fast as I could and joined Heinrich. We pushed the board back over the space. We didn't have a lot of room up there, but it smelled nice from the linden blossoms Tante Berta dried in the attic last summer.

I heard a strange noise, like things getting moved around by the stairs. I tried to get us settled as comfortably as I could, not knowing how long we'd be up there. Heinrich and I got close and wrapped ourselves in the blanket like two caterpillars in a cocoon. After a bit I wasn't sure if I was frozen from the cold or from fear. It was a lot worse being in the dark and not knowing what was going on than being in the middle of it all.

Suddenly, there was a loud banging on the front door. Then, deep voices demanded food and said they knew we were hiding someone. They had to search and if they found any of those "dirty Jews", everyone would be hauled off to jail for questioning. I felt Heinrich's body stiffen. It was hard to hear what my mother and Tante Berta were saying.

There were loud boots stomping through the small house and gruff voices. One said "off to the barn". Then we heard the cellar door slam against the wall, some more boots going farther away, maybe down the stairs. I couldn't imagine how mother and Tante Berta must have felt. They must have been so scared.

"A-choo" Heinrich sneezed. I held my breath. Then I heard another sneeze from downstairs.

Tante Berta said "Ya, that was me." in a loud voice.

Then there was silence. I prayed that Heinrich wouldn't sneeze again. I just wanted those soldiers to go away.

"The attic?" a deep voice questioned.

Some women's voices were muffled. I prayed harder that they

wouldn't find us. I feared they would be coming up the stairs at any second. I hugged Heinrich tighter.

Then we heard more boots stomping. Maybe they were going out the back door, I hoped. Heinrich and I stayed still and quiet, barely breathing. Something was being dragged out the front door. Please don't let it be Tante or Mama I prayed. There were sounds of doors closing, then silence. We could do nothing but wait, and wait. We heard car engines. That was good. But were Tante Berta and mother still downstairs? I stretched my ears. Were they okay?

It seemed like forever, then we heard laughing and things being moved around in the kitchen. When the footsteps came up the stairs, I breathed a sigh of relief. Tante Berta pushed the board aside and I blinked in the light.

"What happened?" I whispered.

"Come down and we'll tell you." Tante Berta shouted up to us.

Heinrich and I felt like we were stuck together, we separated our stiff bodies and crawled out of the blanket, ducking our heads. Heinrich went slowly down the stairs, with Tante Berta helping him. Then it was my turn.

Mama threw her arms around us as soon as our feet were on the floor. She hugged me so hard I thought my ribs were going to crack. We were all relieved and glad to be alive.

"I just knew they were going to find us, how come they didn't come tromping up to the attic?" I ask puzzled.

The two women looked at each other and laughed.

"Because they didn't see the stairs," said Tante Berta grinning.

"Huh? They are right here." I pointed.

"You see, Tante Berta had the great idea to make them look like shelves. We put everything that fit on them, these jars of tomatoes, cups, and all this stuff you see on the table. Not a one of the soldiers was smart enough to realize that it was a ladder. When they didn't see one, they forgot about the attic.

They were in such a hurry to find food in the cellar and I think they were convinced that whoever we were supposed to be hiding was in the barn, that they never even looked up. Even when one of you sneezed, Berta sneezed right away and convinced them that it was her."

"Don't give me all the credit, Hildegard. You helped and the children were quiet, even though they must have been shivering up there."

"I was so afraid they had killed you and dragged your bodies out the door, cause we heard sounds like that."

"Oh, Heidemarie, that wasn't us thank goodness. But it was almost all of our food from the cellar."

Tante Berta lit a candle, opened the cellar door, and went downstairs. She was gone only a few minutes. When she came back, her head was hanging and she wiped her tears with her apron.

Mother put her arm around her.

Between sniffles, Tante Berta said, "They took everything, everything except the one bag of beets in the far corner. That's all we have to eat for the rest of the winter."

Mother comforted and reassured her that we'd survive. We were all still alive and that was no small feat, in these times. The four of us hugged and said a prayer.

Chapter Twenty-Seven

Madison Wisconsin 1981

It was Christmastime and Heidi invited me to her house for dinner. Jack opened the door and took the wine and some homemade gingerbread cookies from me. The smell of smoked meat and baking bread reminded me of Sunday at Grandma's house so many years ago. When I came into the kitchen, it felt strange to have a red and green tablecloth instead of the usual mauve one. Jack was happy to have someone else here, since his 22 year-old son was just killed in a motorcycle accident. I didn't know whether to say anything about it or not.

Heidi put a platter of Kasseler Rippchen (pork chops) and sauerkraut on the table. She took a loaf of fresh bread out of the oven and put the mashed potatoes in a bowl. Jack poured the wine and joked that I could have as much as I wanted since I wouldn't be driving. We all laughed.

We sat down and Jack said a prayer.

"God, we thank you for the food before us and the opportunity to be together. We are grateful for a friend to share our blessings, and pray for those who can't be with us today. We ask

your protection and guidance today and all the rest of our days.
Amen."

We served ourselves and everything tasted as good as it
smelled.

"Oh I forgot something," Heidi said as she jumped up from
the table. She went to the fridge and got the cottage cheese, put it in a
big bowl and brought it to the table.

I laughed.

"What's so funny about forgetting the cottage cheese?" Jack
asked.

"Oh, it's that my grandmother always said if you have cottage
cheese for your potatoes, you are rich."

Jack lifted his wine glass and said, "Here's to cottage cheese!
Here's to wealth!"

"…and health and happiness!" Heidi added.

Heidi said this was her favorite meal, especially with pound
cake for dessert. When you do without for so long, it made these
simple meals all the more wonderful.

Jack talked of Christmases past in the army, in the islands of
the Pacific, and in Germany. He met Heidi one night with a group of
Army buddies walking down the street looking for a bar. She and her
friend were going back to Elena's house when one of the guys
grabbed Heidi by the arm. She wanted no part of him and started to
struggle. Jack yelled at him and said he shouldn't behave that way,
especially since he wasn't even drunk. Heidi was overwhelmed that a

soldier would stand up for her in front of his buddies. As they walked on Jack and Heidi fell farther behind the group until Jack finally ended up walking her home.

"Every time Jack got off base after that, you can guess where he was!" Heidi finished the story.

Jack reached over, took her hand and kissed it.

"When my wife Mary died in 1959, I thought I'd never get over it. She left me a great son, John Jr. Now he's gone too. But I still have my Heidi."

After dinner Jack went to nap in his easy chair in the living room, and Heidi and I talked as we cleaned up the kitchen.

Chapter Twenty-Eight

Mannheim 1945

The war dragged on and on. Life was boring. I had read every book in the house at least three times. We ate little and looked like Halloween ghosts. Heinrich was sick, coughing night and day, and mother spent a lot of time making him tea from roots. She wanted to barter with the neighbors for honey and eggs, but Tante Berta wouldn't let her. In those times, you never knew who you could trust. Everyone was trying to survive themselves and if they thought that tattling on you would get them something, they'd do it without thinking twice. People had forgotten how to be kind, and to care about one other. That's what was so awful about the war. People became disconnected. Friends were lost and neighbors weren't there for each other. Families were torn apart.

But spring came, and so did hope. Tante Berta said that maybe this year, they'd have potatoes. She did manage to get some eyes in the marketplace that week. Of course, there would be beets and onions. The onions came up all by themselves every year.

It was Palm Sunday. I felt like we should be getting all dressed up and going to church. But we didn't even do that anymore.

Besides we didn't have any nice clothes, and my shoes were way too small. I wore an old pair of Tante Berta's with rags stuffed in the toes. Just looking at them made me miss Papa even more. Mother promised that life would get better. I doubted it, so many years had been spent trying to eke out a living here, just the four of us. I thought about how wonderful it would have been to go back to school and to have friends again; I wouldn't even mind the studying and the tests.

"Mama, when will this stupid war be over?" I asked, wishing she would tell me 'tomorrow'.

"Soon, Meine Heidele, soon."

"The Russians moved into Poland in January. Maybe Hitler is losing this war." Tante Berta added.

"But isn't that bad? I mean we're German, don't we want to win?" I asked.

"It's more complicated than that; remember Hitler was the one who started all this in the first place. He was a man who would stop at nothing to make himself important, to go down in history. It's too bad he didn't die when the people of Mannheim pushed him off his pedestal on the second story of the town hall that day," mother explained.

I remembered that, but didn't think I really understood what was going on or what the consequences could have been.

"Mama, was it Hitler who bombed our town?"

"No one can prove it, but I wouldn't be surprised. When

Hitler shouted that Mannheim would pay, he meant it. That officer with the awful red mark on the side of his face above his eye, gave us a look that was enough to convince me," mother added.

We talked little as we went about our daily chores. Mother stepped outside to shake out the rag rug, and came back in with a huge smile on her face and a dance in her step. I hadn't seen her this happy in years.

"My, my! What good a little spring sunshine has done for you, Hildegard!" Tante Berta noticed, too.

"My husband is coming! Alfons! He's coming home!" mother was overcome with joy.

"Did you see him on the road?" Tante Berta asked.

"Oh, no, but I'm sure he's on his way. He'll be here by Easter," she was certain.

"Don't count on it, Dear. I know it's been an awful time, especially this last winter. But I guess it's a good thing to have hope," Tante Berta said.

Then she took me by the arm and gently guided me into the kitchen as mother continued to clean the living room floor.

"Heidemarie, I think you mother is starting to go crazy. Don't take her too seriously. With Bertram and your father gone, then your home and the store. She's been so afraid of losing Heinrich too. It's all been too much for her. Just try to be kind to her and let her have her hope. She needs it to hang on."

I just nodded my head, trying to understand how mother could seem so convinced when she didn't even have a shred of evidence.

A few days later I was in the yard with mother digging up sassafras roots. She got a strange look on her face, staring off into the distance.

"Mama, are you okay?" I asked.

"Ya, everything is fine. It will be just fine. You'll see."

Was Mama going crazy? I knew Tante Berta thought so. But we had to let her have hope.

"Okay" was all I could say as I kept digging at the piece of root mother cut free.

#

On Easter Sunday, we gathered, just the four of us, in the living room and prayed. Tante Berta went into the kitchen, and brought a pan of buns out of the oven. I thought I had smelled something wonderful when we were praying, and was sure it was just my imagination. Heinrich jumped up and down clapping his hands, like a little kid. He was so genuinely happy, it made me feel good too. I thought, if Jesus could rise from the dead, maybe Germany could too.

We ate our buns with sassafras tea, savoring every delicious bite. A huge banquet couldn't have been more satisfying. Heinrich grinned so much it took him a while to finish eating. I wondered if Mama's dream would come true, but I didn't dare say a word about father coming, for fear that would have jinxed it. We picked up every crumb and left one bun on the plate. Silently we all hoped that father really would come to eat it.

Mother went to the front window; she stood there and waited and waited. I prayed that she wasn't going crazy. Suddenly, she rushed out the front door and ran down the road. Tante Berta, Heinrich and I hurried to the door. We saw a very thin man with a scraggly beard coming toward us. Mother's apron and skirt were flying until they met and threw their arms around each other. For a few long minutes they were frozen in a hug.

"Ach du Himmel! It must be Papa!"

When they got back to the house he hugged and kissed Heinrich and me, he told us how much he had missed us and how big we had grown. We asked about Onkel Hansi and Bertram.

"I got separated from them a few years ago, but an old friend from Mannheim told me that he saw Bertram a few months ago, and so we have reason to hope he'll make it back from the war soon. As for Hansi, well, we can only pray and hope he'll return too," Papa told us.

I pinched myself, thinking this was all a dream. I never would have recognized Papa, being so thin and with that yucky beard. But his voice was the same as I remembered it. Tante Berta brought him the last bun and we truly rejoiced on that Easter Sunday, the first day of April, the first day we truly knew that life would go on. Little did we know how much work it would be to get back to normal.

Chapter Twenty-Nine

Madison Wisconsin 1982

At work, there were sirens. I rushed to the front of the building only to see them carrying Heidi out on a stretcher. I asked to go in the ambulance with her, and asked if anyone had called Jack. No one answered me, so I just climbed in the back with Heidi. As the vehicle darted around the beltline highway to the hospital, EMTs were prodding and sticking needles into Heidi. When we arrived, they practically pushed me out onto the ground as the stretcher was wheeled into the emergency room. Doctors and nurses converged on the stretcher with Heidi's limp body and her pale face. Amidst all the commotion, I heard the words 'brain aneurysm', and looked around for Jack, then squeezed my way to Heidi's side and grabbed her ice-cold hand.

Softly, I whispered over and over "Heidi you can't let go, not yet. Jack needs you."

It was almost as if I had talked myself into a trance. I was barely aware of anyone else around me, just white everywhere. Then I heard Jack's voice.

"Oh, yeah, she's her sister. C'mon they are whisking her off to surgery, I just signed the papers," Jack said as he pulled my arm away and I let Heidi's hand fall onto the gurney.

#

Hours passed as Jack and I sat. All our wonderful talks at Heidi's table ran through my mind. How I loved listening to her voice with the familiar German accent.

"Let's go get some coffee and dinner in the cafeteria here. I know it's not Perkins, but it'll have to do. I'm paying; for you to be here with us means a lot," Jack said.

I followed him down the never-ending corridors toward the smell of food. A pork chop and sauerkraut was my choice, I knew it would have been Heidi's too. We didn't say much and I barely noticed Jack eating. We returned to the surgical waiting area and time became an illusion. Finally, a doctor came out and said they managed to stop the bleeding and Heidi was stable. In about an hour they were going to take her from recovery to ICU (the intensive care unit in the hospital). We decided to go and get some sleep since it would be a few days before Heidi would be aware of anything. Jack drove me back to work to get my car and I went home.

After a week, I was allowed to see Heidi. She smiled weakly and the bandage on her head looked like a huge turban. I asked what she remembered.

"Only a little… a sudden horrific headache and then feeling like I was falling, sirens, and your hand. You were whispering something to me. I thought you told me I couldn't go because I still had to finish my story about my life in Germany."

"That wasn't what I was saying. I was telling you that you couldn't go yet, that Jack needed you," I replied.

"But you do want to hear the rest of the story, I know," Heidi said.

"Hmm, actually, you're right. I keep trying to figure out how your mother knew that your father would be home for Easter."

"If I live to be 100, I'll never *really* know. I believe that there's a magical connection between some people, sort of like a special intuition. There was always something between my parents. They'd finish each other's sentences and ask the same question at the same time. We're all connected at some higher level, but there are people who are more aware of it than others. As soon as I get out of this place, I'll finish our story over linden tea at the kitchen table," Heidi promised.

Chapter Thirty

Mannheim 1946-48

Heidi keeps her promise and continues…

After the war, we thought things would be better. Bertram came home, too old for school and left with the choice of working on the farm with Tante Berta or following in his father's footsteps as a shoemaker. Onkel Hansi never made it back from the war.

My father had to re-build his shop and our home. Papa, Bertram and I made the trek back to Mannheim with knapsacks of food, water and a few tools. In the daylight, what was our lovely town center was a huge pile of rubble. My heart sank.

Bertram said sadly, "maybe we should look for another town to start a shoe store in."

"Nein. Mannheim is our home," Papa answered.

"How will we *ever* be able to rebuild this?" I asked in disbelief.

"One brick and one stone at a time. Now, let's get started." Papa said as he began piling stones on one side, bricks in the middle and wood on the other side. We followed his example. It was hard work and very tiring. No one else was around. Gertrut and the friends I used to play with had no homes either. They were only ghosts. As we moved building materials out of the way, we'd find a treasure, a pot, a jar of tomatoes, or a fork where the kitchen used to be. We'd dust these off and set them to the side. Father took some wood and made a huge box, big enough for four people to get in.

"What are you doing?" I asked curiously.

"Making us a shelter to sleep in. This place isn't going to be done in a day, and we can't waste precious time walking back and forth to Neuhofen every day."

"You mean, we are going to sleep here? Can't we sleep in the cellar?"

"Ya, we are sleeping here. If you can find the door to the cellar and are sure it hasn't collapsed, maybe we could sleep there, but this will have to do for now. Let's keep working, Heidemarie."

Soon I uncovered a book, Mama's cookbook. I sat on the ground and flipped through it. On one page was a recipe for pound cake.

"Wow! Look at this! A whole pound of butter! Where would you ever get a whole pound of butter?"

"Heidemarie, you must be hungry. I am too. Let's take a break for lunch." Papa said.

"Did Mama ever make this pound cake? Where ever did she get the butter?" I persisted.

"Ah, Heidemarie, you don't remember much from before the

war, do you?"

"I remember school, Gertrut, and my other friends and eating other foods besides beets, beets and more beets." I replied.

"Well, things will get better, you'll see. You'll be back in school soon, and the smart girl that you are, you'll do well, too."

Bertram ate sitting on a large rock with a far-away look on his thin face.

Soon we were back at picking through the rubble and sorting it. It must have been a lot worse than when we left it years ago, after rains and snows. We worked until dark. I was almost too tired to eat anything. Father found a clear spot and then he and Bertram put our shelter there. We three climbed in with an old blanket and tried to sleep. I heard strange noises, hoot owls, and rats running on top of our box. I wanted to go back to the farm. I hardly slept all night; I dreamt of huge rats talking about us being dead and trying to eat us. The next day we were all tired, but we worked hard. Luckily the rats didn't get our food.

On the third day, father said we could go back to the farm a few hours before dark. We were dragging by then and I couldn't wait to go. When we got back, Heinrich was sick. So Mama decided that Bertram and I would take turns working with Papa while the other stayed to help with the farm work and Heinrich. Papa took a day off and then he and Bertram went back to Mannheim for another three days.

At first I was dreading my turn. But then it was like a treasure hunt. After a month or so a few other families came back and started re-building. Every day I hoped to see Gertrut again. This went on for the rest of the spring and the whole summer. A big milestone was getting running water again. One night when Bertram and Papa came home, they announced that the whole first floor was finished and the upstairs was one big room, but all covered. We could move back to Mannheim before the winter for sure.

Oh what a happy day, October 1st! We used the old horse wagon and loaded it with stuff. A neighbor of Tante Berta's loaned us two horses and soon we were unloading things into the house.

And Tante Berta... well Onkel Hansi never came back and we couldn't leave her alone in Neuhofen. So Tante Berta decided to sell the farm and she moved to Mannheim with us. In the next year, other houses were rebuilt, some new people came to town and made shops and homes where our Jewish neighbors used to be. Papa got his shoe store open with some of the shoes he made before the war. He and Bertram unearthed them, cleaned and polished them and sold shoes again. Papa was pleased that Bertram was getting to be good at sewing leather and he especially liked making boots. Even Heinrich helped; he loved to polish shoes.

Tante Berta missed the farm, but she was excited when she uncovered an old sack of potatoes that had sprouted in the cellar. In the spring, she planted the whole space behind our house in potatoes. I went to school and you'll never guess who was there! It was so good to see my old friend Gertrut. Her father died in the war and her family had lost everything. Her mother got sick with consumption and passed on too. So she lived with her older brother and his wife on a farm nearby.

I had lots of friends, and studied hard, especially science and math. Papa and Mama promised me a pound cake when I graduated, which was such a happy day, second only to that Easter Sunday when Papa came home.

Chapter Thirty-One

Madison Wisconsin 1982

We sat in Heidi's kitchen, watching the snowflakes fall.

"So that sounds like everything got back to normal in a few years, you finished school, met Jack, got married and came to America to live happily ever after with all the pound cake you could bake."

"Well, it wasn't quite that simple. One night the whole family had gone to Heidelberg but me. The most popular boy in my class was jealous of me because I was smarter than him. But he was charming. He asked me out on a date, which was rare as most kids always partied and stayed in groups. But we had a few drinks alone and when he took me home, one thing led to another and we were in bed together. He tried to convince me that nothing ever happened the first time. I'd had just enough to drink that I didn't have any sense."

"So what happened then?"

"I found out I was pregnant. My father was furious and forbade me to see him again. Bertram became my protector and bodyguard. My friends deserted me. But some good came of it. The baby was a boy and we named him Johann, called him Hansi, which made Tante Berta happy.

Heinrich loved playing with him, and Tante Berta and mother took care of him during the day. My parents insisted I stay in school, saying that education was something no one could take away from you. It was hard without any friends, but when I came home and did my homework, little Hansi sat and watched me. The only trouble he ever made was that he loved to take out the pots and pans and crawl under the kitchen cabinet. One day we discovered a pencil hidden in there and pictures of tiny cars he'd drawn.

When I finished school, we celebrated with champagne and pound cake, of course! I got a job in a lab at the Hochschule Mannheim and was able to take classes for free. I loved the work and was always learning something new. I bought all our groceries and contributed to the household. Life was good and we all enjoyed watching Hansi grow up. When he was 17, he went away to Art school. A year later I met Jack, married him and came to America in 1964. My parents gave me their blessing. It was hard, I still miss them and especially Heinrich and Hansi, but I knew it was time for me to make a new life and I loved Jack and he loved me. Hansi went on to a very successful career as a graphic artist; he got married and has two lovely children."

"So, the moral of the story is: always have hope, get an education, be happy, make your success, and enjoy pound cake!" Heidi concluded.

PART III

NOTHING IS FOREVER

Chapter Thirty-Two

Brookline Massachusetts 1987

On Valentine's Day, my fiancé took me to meet his parents. We entered the charming brownstone and climbed three long flights up to their apartment in the dim light. As we were going up, he warned me that he had brought many, many girls to meet his mother through the years, and she had never approved of a one.

"But, don't worry, that won't keep me from marrying you," he said.

I hesitated. My hand was shaking as I knocked softly on the door. My fiancé laughed, reached around me, and knocked loudly. I was frozen, thinking how important it would be to get along with my future mother-in-law; I really wanted her to like me.

This little blond lady opened the door and threw her arms around me as I stepped over the threshold. She pulled me inside; her strength amazed me. Startled, I gasped. Sofia apologized telling me it was bad luck to stand on the threshold. After a quick "come in", she led me down a long hallway lined with bookshelves. There was an archway to the living room on the right, a dining room filled with boxes of papers on the left and a cheery kitchen in the far back of the apartment. I couldn't help but feel strange in this old place with all the clutter. There were even bottles of motor oil and antifreeze on a cart in the kitchen.

We sat down on green vinyl and chrome chairs. An orange and blue flowered tablecloth jumped out at me. Nothing matched and my eyes were accosted by a visual cacophony, so different from my own organized, coordinated lifestyle. Sofia busied herself making coffee and serving us an array of pastries fit for royalty, all on mismatched pieces of china and fun mugs with sayings on them, like "Believe you can" and "You're the berries."

A burly fellow walked into the room; quietly he reached out his huge hand to me, and introduced himself as Chaim.

When we shook, I thought he was going to crush every bone in my right hand. I knew he must be in his 70s, but he could have easily passed for 50. He teased his wife, Sofia, claiming she hadn't fed him in two days. As he took a seat next to my fiancé, he gave me a warm smile and his brown eyes sparkled with mischief. There was a clear resemblance between the two handsome men across the table. Sofia slipped into speaking Yiddish and then apologized to me, saying she knew it was not polite. My response was that it was fine to speak in Yiddish as long as they knew I understood about 80% of what they were saying. So the conversation continued in a comfortable mix of the two languages. We spent about an hour laughing, talking, eating and drinking.

#

Two years passed, we were married, bought a house, and our daughter was born. I decided that I had waited long enough and quit my job to stay home with her. One of the best parts of this decision was Wednesday afternoons, when I took the baby and visited Sofia, the baby's grandmother, who we started calling Savta (Grandma in Hebrew). Her husband (Chaim) died a few months before the baby was born, saying only that his son should have a boy. These Wednesday afternoons were so important to Savta since she had the opportunity to ask me what I thought of her every decision, large or small.

We all had the impression that she was the one who ruled the household, as she handled all the money, did the cooking and shopping, and seemed to be in charge. How wrong we were! She relied on her husband for approval, and it had been very hard for her to go on without him.

She had her own community of friends who hung out at the local McDonalds, went to the senior center for lunch, and took trips. But she spent a lot of time alone, so I brought the baby on Wednesday afternoons and we visited as a family on weekends. These were special times, when her story unfolded.

Chapter Thirty-Three

Riga, Latvia 1939-1941

One Wednesday afternoon, Savta begins her story...

Finally things were getting better for my family. Father was a kind man, worked as a machinist, and had seven children with my mother. The oldest, Moshe was 18 when I was born. Father went blind when I was only four. A piece of metal shot out of the machine he was working on and lodged in his eye; infection set in. Soon it had spread to the other eye. Moshe and Eda were married by then. Abbie, Robert and Genia were old enough to help out, so the family managed. Then, by some miracle, father's eyesight came back after almost ten years of blindness! We were amazed! He got a job in the shop again, as the owner remembered what a good worker he had been. With things unsettled in Europe, machined parts were going to be needed more and more, even though Latvia hoped to stay out of any war.

In 1939, our Polish neighbors were attacked. Rumors about Jews began to spread. My parents worried. When it was time to go to school in September of 1940, my mother said I wasn't going. What?

They both valued education so much and I loved school. Being the youngest, all my sisters and brothers taught me things before it was part of my classes, so I was very smart and wanted to become a doctor. I couldn't understand; I begged for an answer, and became unruly. My mother asked me to be good, that soon I would know.

A week passed. Before father left for work, I hugged everyone and then my mother gave me her large cloth bag, hugged me tightly, and told me to follow a path through the forest in Rumbala.

"Look for a large, white building with a cross on it. That is the convent. You must go and knock on the door; a lady in strange clothes will come and take you in. It's all arranged. You see darling Sofia, it is not safe for Jews in our city anymore. You are beautiful with blond hair and blue eyes; you have a chance, and the rest of us do not. We look Jewish, and it will be awful for us. You must go and be strong my little one. I'll be with you, I promise."

I looked back at her sad brown eyes, urging me on.

"Now Go!" my Emma (Mama) said, hugging me tightly, and then pushing me away.

I knew that would be the last time I'd ever see her face, but I turned and walked away obediently.

As I got into the forest, I still heard her voice calling me, "Sofia, Sofia, you must go."

Then I heard footsteps behind me. At first I thought mother was following me. As they came closer, I realized they were too heavy, like boots. I didn't dare turn to look. I just began running faster and faster. The boots came running after me. A hand grabbed my arm and in a moment I was face to face with a soldier. He said nothing. I froze and stared into his eyes. He turned his head and there was this horrible red growth on the side of his face, just above his eye. I imagined it growing until he turned into a horrid red monster. I was so frightened that I yanked my arm out of his and took off running. He stood there, for some reason he didn't come after me. I'll never know why. But I kept on running hearing my mother's voice calling my name all the way to the building she had described. I almost collapsed at the door and dropped my bag. It took every ounce of strength to stand and knock hard on the big wooden door.

A lady in a long black dress opened the door and said in a soft voice, "you poor tired, child, we've been expecting you. Come in. Come in, quickly!"

She picked up my bag, pulled me over the threshold and closed the huge wooden door. I sat down on the floor, my legs felt like rubber and my chest was heaving in and out. She stood there for a few minutes and told me that they had no more beds, but I'd be safe and warm here in the convent. After a bit, I got up and looked in the bag. On top was a loaf of fresh bread with a note in my mother's handwriting.

It said:

"Dear Sisters,

This is our youngest child, Sofia. She is our only hope. I

know you will take care of her and do whatever is best. Please take this bread as a small token of our thanks. Esther."

I handed the bread to the Sister, and again heard my mother's voice saying my name.

After a few weeks, the Mother Superior took me to a quiet space and sat me down. She told me that they were afraid for my safety, even in the convent. They were trying to get me a passport so I could go to Russia and get away from the Nazis. They told me that all the Nazi soldiers were mean and did awful things, especially to Jews.

"Never let them know you are Jewish; while you are here we will teach you enough about Catholicism and a few prayers so you can pretend if you have to. Dear, you must be strong. We have faith and will pray for you. You will survive, God has blessed you," the Mother Superior told me and I never forgot her words.

Chapter Thirty-Four

Brookline, Massachusetts 1989

As I dragged myself, the baby, diaper bag and the umbrella stroller up the three long flights of stairs, it seemed as if they went on forever. Two of the lights in the stairwell were burnt out, so it felt like I was climbing Mount Everest, cautiously, one step at a time. Finally I got to the door at the top and knocked loudly. In a minute I heard metal moving on the other side. Then Savta swung the door open and I saw the bar and two deadbolts. She took the baby as I dropped everything else on the floor.

"You poor dear! You look exhausted!" Here, take a nap on the couch," she said as she ushered me into the living room and pulled a colorful afghan off the back.

"While you nap, I'll take the baby for a walk," she continued as she grabbed the stroller and headed down the stairs. I collapsed on the couch, suddenly realizing how tired I was.

When I awoke I heard someone rattling at the door. I bolted upright and then realized that it was Savta. She set the stroller by the door and brought the sleeping baby in. Now that was the definition of peaceful, you could almost see a halo and a little smile on the baby's face. Savta was glowing with happiness.

"Everyone I saw said she looks just like me!" Savta exclaimed proudly as she arranged a blanket on the floor and lay the baby down.

"Oh you look so much better rested. Let's have some coffee and pastries. I made Kreplach (Jewish raviolis) this morning, so be sure to take some home with you."

We went into the kitchen and I sat at the table. Savta made coffee and got cheese rolls and apricot-filled pastries. I couldn't decide which to take, so I had half of each. They were good, but not quite the same as the fresh ones Sabba (Chaim) used to make.

I began our conversation with questions, "So, how did you get out of Latvia? And how did you meet Sabba?"

Chapter Thirty-Five

From Riga, Latvia to Siberia 1941-1944

One day at the convent, one of the sisters came and said we must go to get me a passport. I was happy to go outside, but afraid I would see that scary soldier again. The nun must have understood my hesitation and told me she'd go with me. When we got to the government building, an official took my paper and asked a lot of questions, most of which the sister answered for me. Then he told us to come back in three months.

On the way back to the convent, I saw signs in the streets that said awful lies about Jews. I wanted tear them down and scream, but the sister held my hand tightly and pulled me away from them. When we got to the forest, I watched around every tree expecting to see the scary soldier waiting for me. A few people passed us and some others went our way, but nothing more happened.

It was a quiet life for the next few months, especially after Mother Superior had taken my blanket and told me to get my things and follow her. She opened this large wooden door and we went into a small hallway and then downstairs. The walls had alcoves that were evenly spaced. I reached my hand out as we walked and felt tiny little bumps that had been painted a pale yellow-brown.

We finally came to an open room. One wall was lined with shelves full of wine bottles. Mother Superior walked over to the edge and pushed against it. The whole section of shelves moved and there was another large space behind it. Three children sat on a large piece of fur in the middle of the floor. The oldest was a girl about twelve. She shook her curly black hair and her large brown eyes stared at me in the dim light. Mother Superior tapped her on the head and said it was all right; then she introduced me as Sofia.

As I started to say something, I realized that other children were huddled in blankets in the corners of the room. A few were playing with pebbles, and some had little bundles of their own. Everything was bare except for the large cross on the wall with that man they called Jesus hanging on it. It felt really spooky to me, so I tried not to look at the cross. The only light came from an old lamp tucked into a hollowed-out space in the wall on the left.

When Mother Superior turned to go, I ran over and touched her shoulder, not sure what to say. She looked at me kindly and said that I'd be safer here with the other children and she'd be back with food for us all soon. Then she disappeared behind the shelves and there was a wall where we had come in. The brown-eyed girl looked like she was afraid of me. So I tried to be nice to her and asked her name.

"Sarah" was all she said.

Except for when one of the nuns came and brought us food,

we were all alone in the cellar. These kids were not like my brothers
and sisters. They were all quiet and didn't do much of anything.
Maybe they were sad being away from their homes too. We had no
books or toys. A few times this male nun came in dressed in a long
dark brown robe with a hood. At first I thought he was scary, but he
sat with us and told stories about Francis, who loved animals and
Theresa who he called the little flower, and Patrick who tamed snakes
from faraway places like France and Ireland. I had heard of these
places in school, but knew nothing about the people.

I was grateful for food and shelter, but I missed my family;
that hurt so much. My mother's voice called to me at times,
especially when I was trying to go to sleep at night. In the middle of
January, it was very cold, when Sister came down and brought us
food. Then she told me it was time to go get my passport. I took coins
out of the bag that my mother had given me and put them in my
pocket. Then I took all my things and followed the nun upstairs. We
bundled up, left the convent and trudged the long path through the
forest and into the city. The wind was blowing and snow was flying. I
kept my head down to protect my face from the bitter cold. We
waited and waited in a very long line. Finally, the official asked my
name and flipped through a box of light brown cards. He pulled mine
out, looked at the picture and then looked at me. He looked at the
picture again and then yanked the scarf off my head. I put my feet
firmly on the floor, expecting him to slap me across the face.

Sister asked him how much and his eyes brightened. I dug in

my pocket and handed her three coins. He grabbed the coins, stuffed them in his pocket and handed me the card. Sister reached around my shoulder, spun me around and hurried me out the door. She told me to guard that passport with my life. Going back through the forest, we saw lots of footprints in the snow. I was reminded of the soldier with the red monster mark on his face and wondered if some of the prints were from his boots, but sister rushed me along, and I was anxious to get out of the cold too.

Months passed. I missed lighting Shabbat candles, Passover, the city and especially my life with my family. More kids came, and many were younger than me. I tried to comfort them, and this made me feel a little better. The convent was becoming very crowded and the helpings of food kept getting smaller. The summer came and went and I longed to go out and play or just take a walk. It was not safe and we knew it. In September, I wanted to go back to school and see my friends and learn again. I wondered why the world had been turned upside-down.

The end of the month, someone came to the convent. The sisters were all upset. Anyone who could go, had to leave as soon as possible. It wasn't safe here anymore. After I put on almost all the clothes I owned, I took my bag, and packed everything else in it. My instructions were to go to the train station and get myself over the border into Russia. The last thing the Sisters said to me was "God be with you."

Now I was truly alone in this great, big frightening world. As

I walked along I heard my mother's voice calling me and I looked around for her, following the voice to the train station. At the window I got a ticket to Pskov. I kept to myself and clutched my bag all the way.

When the train got to Pskov, the town had been destroyed. The Germans had been there already. The conductor said we were lucky the train tracks were still usable, and we were able to go on to Porkhov and Staraja. A few passengers got off in Pskov. The conductor let them, and then he came around and asked us for more money for coal to keep going. I gave him a coin and he let me stay. The conductor made a few more people get off.

At the next two stops, I hid under the seat so I wouldn't have to give him more money. I fell asleep with my bag under my head as a pillow. I woke up when the train stopped again in some tiny town in Siberia. I heard my mother's voice calling Sofia. I was sure it was real and she was here, so I got off the train and looked for her. I was at least a day and a night away from home and freezing.

It was daylight, so I wandered about the little village. It was nothing like Riga; there were small, ugly one-story buildings and already snow on the ground. The smell of fresh bread was coming form a small building, so I went in. A stocky man asked me if I was the one sent to work there. Of course I said yes, thinking I wouldn't starve to death in a bakery. I told him that I was really good with numbers and could weigh and measure things very well.

He looked at me curiously and said, "hmm, well, I do need an assistant and not just another baker. They keep asking for more and more bread for the troops."

He took a piece of paper and had me add columns of numbers. I did them quickly in my head. He took the paper over to his office and came back about five minutes later. I watched all the ladies who were busy kneading dough and putting loaves on wooden paddles to go into the oven. The boss came out, holding the paper and he was amazed that all my calculations were correct. Of course I was getting to stay as his assistant, and I was careful to be nice to all the women there. It was shelter in a cold and empty place and we had bread, but I missed Riga and my family so much.

Time passed, I kept busy all day weighing and adding, counting up ingredients and loaves of bread. One day two scraggly fellows came in and talked to the boss. One, named Jacob, spoke in broken Russian, but insisted that there was no better baker anywhere. He'd been making bread since he was ten. He wouldn't take "no" for an answer when the boss said all the bakers were women.

Finally, he agreed to test this guy who claimed to be the best. The boss said that if this self-proclaimed baker could make ten loaves of bread to impossible specifications, the boss would let him and his friend stay and work. I weighed out all the ingredients, slipping in a little extra when no one was looking. Jacob set to work with steady hands and a quiet smile. The first snatch of happiness I had seen in this gloomy part of the world since I got here. When his bread came out, it weighed more than the average and the loaves had risen more than any to ever come out of that oven.

After I gave the boss the weights, he looked at me and asked what I thought, "Should we let these two stay?"

I told him yes, firmly, but not too enthusiastically. The deal was that they had to leave for the night so he could think it over and come back in the morning.

I slipped one loaf out of the pile in the back and cut it lengthwise into four pieces. I told the boss I'd see the two men out. Then I pulled the hidden bread out from under my apron and slid it into the sleeves of their coats. If the boss had seen me do that, he would have thrown me out in the cold with nothing. But I was lucky. The two men went back to the train station for shelter for the night.

I slept fitfully. The baker-man, Jacob, had a sad, yet hopeful look in his eyes. He seemed like an honest person. *The boss has to say yes and let them stay*, I thought. When morning came, he told them they had jobs, on these conditions: they would sleep on the bakery floor, they would haul in all the heavy bags of flour and they would work at least 12 hours a day. So that's how I met my husband.

He and his best friend, Michal, went to fight in the Polish army in 1939, but they were no match for the Germans. He told me that they went to war with a saber on each shoulder, a new rifle and no ammunition. When most of their platoon got captured, Jacob and Michal escaped and clung to the bottom of a train for kilometers to escape to Russia, only to be caught by the Russians. The Russian army general was afraid that two adventurous fellows might defect if put on the front lines, so they were put on a train to western Siberia, where they had explicit instructions to report to a factory to make rope for the Russian Navy. Well, Jacob told me they had every intention of following their orders, until he smelled baking bread. Michal then dared him to go into the bakery and get them work, or at least a few pieces of bread.

Things went well for a while, and when the boss left for the day, I'd let Jacob into the office to stay the night with me. We fell in love and forgot the pain and misery of the war, how much we missed our families, and how we'd left normal lives behind in Riga and Bialystok. Soon we learned that nothing is forever.

Chapter Thirty-Six

Brookline, Massachusetts 1989

"Oh Savta, that story is incredible! I could sit and listen all night, but let's tend to this crying baby."

I changed her diaper and fed her. Then we got everything together and Savta helped me get the baby, stroller, diaper bag and Kreplach down the stairs. We hugged and kissed goodbye.

When I drove home, I couldn't seem to get her story out of my head. I told my husband and he said that there was a lot more to come. It seemed that just when you thought it would all turn out well, something else happened. He felt that so many people would have been defeated by the circumstances, or would have been bitter by the hands that fate dealt them. But his parents never stopped hoping and living for the future and for their children. They were true heroes, as were all those who survived the Holocaust and lived with the insanity that surrounded Europe back in those times.

I could hardly wait until next week to hear what happened next. I begged my husband to tell me more, but he said I really needed to hear it from Savta since he was far too young to remember most of the story. I supposed he was right, it was almost as if the orange and blue tablecloth was part of the tale. I should have known that something horrible was about to happen, when Savta said that nothing is forever.

Chapter Thirty-Seven

Siberia 1944

Ah! It was summertime, at least the air was fresh and birds were chirping, although it still felt so much colder than in Riga. My stomach felt strange all the time and I could hardly eat. I thought I was getting a cold, as I was tired all the time. But I was happy and Jacob and I were so much in love. He was so kind to me, and even though he hardly stopped working all day I knew he was watching me.

Usually only a few soldiers came to load up the bread onto jeeps and drive it away. But one afternoon, after all the bread was gone, another jeep pulled up and three soldiers jumped out and came storming into the bakery. One grabbed the boss by the collar and demanded answers. They wanted to know what able-bodied men were doing in a bakery. They were needed for "manly labor".

"Who are these two fellows, anyway?" they wanted to know, " and where are they supposed to be?"

Jacob saw them, gave my hand a quick squeeze and whispered for me to hide behind the desk in the office. I realized that if Jacob even cast me a loving glance, I would be in grave danger. I did as he said, in spite of the fact that I wanted to scream at the soldiers to leave him alone.

There was a scuffle and Michal and Jacob were dragged away by the three soldiers. The boss shoved them out the door; that was probably how he saved himself, shouting that they *did* need a man to run this place. I peeked out the only window in the office just in time for one last glance at my beloved being driven away by more craziness of the war.

That night I cried and cried. I was back to being in a strange land all alone. But this time something was different. I was sure that I was pregnant with his child. I couldn't stay here. To have a baby in the middle of winter in this godforsaken place would have been the worst thing ever.

Chapter Thirty-Eight

Bialystok, Poland 1944-1945

The very next day I planned my escape and tied my bag
beneath my skirt. I told the boss I had to go outside and get a breath
of fresh air. I went out the side door where there were no windows,
and just kept walking all the way to the train station. There was
always a crowd coming and going. I mixed in easily and found the
next train heading west. I got a ticket, thankful for all the coins my
mother sewed into my coat and bag. I got back to what was once my
home. Riga was demolished. My home, my city was empty, except
for a few stray animals. I saw no one. Instantly, I knew my whole
family was dead, gone. Mother was right. She knew.

I ran back through the woods, hoping to find the convent, but
the walls were all crumbled and no one was there either. I sat on the
step and cried. I cried for the kind Sisters, for all the little Jewish
children, for my whole family, for the city. Then I heard my mother's
voice calling softly "Sofia, Sofia…Sofia." I stood up and looked all
around. Nothing but silence, no one, not a footstep. I wandered into
what used to be the convent and found a few blankets with moth

holes, broken dishes, a candlestick and then the stairs to the cellar. I pushed the door open and decided that this would do for shelter for the night. I took the candlestick for protection and wrapped myself in the blankets. I felt as if my mother was with me, so I managed to drift off to sleep. Early the next morning, I awakened and gathered up my things.

Over the next few weeks, as if in a trance, I made my way from one train station to another from Daugavpils to Vilnius to Grodno. Now I knew I was getting close to the Polish border. So I got off and followed the railroad tracks from a distance, staying away from anyplace where there might be someone to question me. Day and night I traveled on foot, made sure that I heard the trains and didn't stray too far from railroad tracks.

Finally I saw the ruins of what once was a large city. Like Riga, it certainly wasn't a city for living, but I thought I might find someone who knew of my husband's family. I wandered about, pretending I knew where I was, trying to remember every description Jacob had given me, as I repeated over and over the names of his seven brothers and sisters. In the center of what looked like a walled off section of the city, I found a building with a large brick oven inside.

I knew this must have been a bakery. I felt that Jacob was here, the smell almost lingered. Poking around I lost myself, imagining what this once looked like when Jacob lived here with his family, when they got up every morning and started making bread, bagels and rolls. I rummaged through the piles of rubble and found an old chest, which I pried open with a piece of railing. In it was a beautiful lace cloth, some pictures, an Old Testament and two prayer shawls. I fumbled through the pictures and found one of Jacob with what must have been his family around a table, a portrait of Jacob and a few more pictures, probably his siblings. I stuffed the picture of him and a few others in my bag.

Suddenly, I was aware of footsteps behind me. I froze. There was no place to hide. I held my breath, afraid to turn around. Someone came and gently tapped me on the shoulder.

"Looking for someone?" the raspy voice of an old woman asked.

I turned and looked at her, dressed in ragged clothes, and wondered if I could trust her.

"Who are you?" I replied with a question.

"My name's Marta, but that doesn't matter. This used to be my city, now it is nothing. I hid in a wine cellar, hearing shouts, screams of fire, gunshots, and children crying. After three days, I finally came out and found every Jewish person I knew gone, some dead in the streets. I found myself in a strange world. Even the synagogue on Suraska Street was burnt to the ground. I managed to scrounge and keep alive hiding in this wreckage of a city. I've answered your question, now what's your story?"

"I came to find someone, anyone from my husband's family, the bakers here."

"Oh, Dearie, I am so sorry. They are all gone. Most of the family died in the synagogue fire when the Nazis sealed off the doors while Jews were inside praying. The father of the family was in the hospital at the time, with a broken arm. Even there it wasn't safe. All the Jews were put on the eighth floor, and then thrown out the windows to fall to their deaths. Now tell me, where is your husband?"

"The Russians took him away from the bakery in Siberia and that was the last I saw of him. My family in Riga is all gone. I hoped to find a relative of my husband's here. You see I am carrying his baby. I have no place else to go." My voice cracked as I tried to hold back the tears.

"Well, I haven't much. But I've managed to survive here by knowing who to trust and when and where to hide. I will do what I can for you and the baby."

"Thank you."

She took me to a small room behind a burned up section of the ghetto and we made another bed from what she had scrounged in the remains of the city. There was an old rectory where two priests still lived. She took me there and we bartered some rag rugs she'd made for food. As it got colder we stacked up wood, we could burn it in the old fireplace in our room, but only at night. We couldn't chance anyone seeing the smoke in the daytime. Marta took care of me and worried about the baby as if she had been my own mother.

One night, the pains started. She boiled water and helped me through the labor and the birth. The baby came, a little boy. I named him Benesh after my father. Oh how I longed to show him to Jacob, my mother, my father, and my whole family. I hugged the precious bundle and he made me very happy. Marta loved him too and said we all deserved some joy in a time like this. I gave her the last possession that my mother had packed in my bag almost four years ago, a beautiful handmade green sweater. She bartered it for a sheet, which I tore up to make diapers for my baby.

A few months later, word came that the Germans were losing the war. In the spring, we heard the Russians were marching on Berlin. Next, the news was that Hitler had committed suicide. What a coward! The war in Germany was over before summer. The priests told Marta that parts of Germany were being given back to Poland, and some surviving Jews were going to Dzierzoniow. I decided that was where I must go. Before I left, I made sure everyone in Marta's trusted network knew where I would be, so that when Michal and Jacob returned, they would know where to find me.

Chapter Thirty-Nine

From Bialystok to Dzierzoniow 1945

The baby was seven months old when we boarded a train to cross Poland. It was summer and we saw some green fields on our way from Bialystok to Warsawa to Zgierz to Lodz to Kalicz. We were barreling into Wroclaw.

BOOM! Crash! The train stopped. Metal was flying all over. People were screaming. I looked down. My right side was stinging; blood was everywhere. The baby cried out loudly. He was bleeding from his side and his leg. I tore my skirt and wrapped his leg and mine. I put pressure on his side to try to stop the bleeding. The only thought going through my mind was that this baby *had* to live. He was all I had.

I managed to get to the nearest hospital. After waiting and waiting, a tall, hefty nurse came out and brought us into this huge room where the walls were lined with cribs. She put my baby on a table in the center, and took off the bloody wrappings. When she picked him up, the poor infant couldn't even hold his head up. She took him to an empty crib.

Then the nurse turned to me and said, "you are young and

beautiful. You'll have more children. You should leave him with us and just forget about him."

I tried to get to his crib and get him out of there, but she blocked my way and pushed me to the door. I pretended that I left, but I waited in the hallway and saw a door on the opposite wall. I waited quietly until I saw that nurse put on her coat. Then I slipped into the crib-lined room, grabbed my little baby boy and rushed out the other door. A cool breeze caught us, and I just kept going as fast as I could to the closest houses. A lady was outside a little wooden house.

"Can you help me?" I asked in my best Polish.

She looked at me suspiciously.

"We were on the train that blew up and my baby is hurt badly."

"Then take him to the hospital," she replied.

"They won't help me."

"So what do you expect me to do?"

"Boil some water so I can cover his wounds properly and a little food would be so helpful," I answered trying to keep my pleading voice from shaking.

"Well, I suppose I could. I haven't much, but you have even less. God said 'Whatever you do for these the least of my brethren you do for me.'"

Being unable to think of anything that the Sisters taught me, I simply answered, "Ah, thank you. You are such a good Christian."

She opened the door to her simple little cabin, and put her arm out for me to enter. She stoked the stove, and put on a kettle of water. I sat in a wooden chair by the table, and suddenly realized how tired I was. Carefully, setting the baby on the table, I kept my arms around him. He seemed listless and tired too. After we cleaned up the baby, she took a clean man's shirt and tore it to make bandages.

"Oh, Dear, don't tear your husband's shirt for me."

"Doesn't matter, he was killed in the war...my two sons as well. I am all alone now. So if I can help you save your son, I will," she said as tears streamed down her face.

I stayed with her almost a week. Her soup was good, with cabbage, onions, beets and potatoes from her small garden. As I got some of my strength back, the baby finally started to nurse again. The next day was Sunday and I feared that she would expect me to go to church with her. I needed to keep my Jewish identity secret. So I told her I needed to be on my way to Dzierzoniow.

"But why? Why there? I heard that Jews who survived are going to that town. Certainly that's reason enough for you not to want to go there!"

"My husband had a relative in Reichenbach, which I understand is now Dzierzoniow and if he survived the war, we planned to meet there," I said with a straight face so I didn't get her suspicious again.

"Well, Dear, I understand. Family is so important. Godspeed and I'll pray for you and the baby."

"Thank you! Thank you again for everything," I said as I held the baby tight with my bag over my shoulder.

I was relieved that she didn't figure out my Jewish identity, but scared since I hadn't a clue where my next meal would come from or who I could trust. It was about 60 kilometers, so I started out walking, following the road, hearing my mother's voice calling "Sofia". A farmer stopped and asked where I was going and if I'd like a ride. At first I hesitated, but he seemed to be a kindly old fellow with sun-wrinkled skin. The farmer's boney hands held the reins to a skinny horse pulling the wagon. He told me that it was a long way to Dzierzoniow. He was going to Bielawa.

"Bielawa?" I had never heard of that place. I was hoping this was good.

"Used to be Langenbielau when it was still Germany, one of the first places where Hitler Youth parades started.

"How close is it to Dzierzoniow?" I asked trying to cover my ignorance.

"About seven kilometers further down the road, so I'm not going out of my way," he said as he jumped down and gave me a hand.

After he helped me up into the wagon, I got comfortable on the hay, cradling the baby in my arms for the long, bumpy ride. This was certainly better than walking. He stopped in Niemcza, went into a building, and brought out a sack of corn. Then he unloaded half of the hay. I sat wondering if I should get out, who he was talking to, if it was still safe to stay with him, how much farther it was to Dzierzoniow, and why he mentioned Hitler Youth parades. He came out and soon we were on our way. When we arrived, he asked for an address and I told him that this small apartment building was fine and I thanked him.

"Well, take care of yourself Ma'am and that cute little bundle you've got there," he said helping me down. I watched his cart until it was out of sight. Then I asked the next person I saw where the convent was. He pointed me to a street that went up a hill. I followed it, looking for any building with a cross on it.

I was tired, and when I got there, they offered me water and asked how they could help. I told them that I was looking for information, for anyone from Bialystok. They sent me to an apartment building on Rezeznicza Street. There I found an old lady from Bialystok on the third floor. She told me her friend worked at a clothing factory. I might be able to get work there and she could take care of the baby if I shared my salary with her. The apartment across the hall was empty and she would talk the landlord into renting it to me if I had any money. I opened the last of the pockets my mother sewed coins into in my bag. She took me to the landlord and talked to him convincingly in Polish. He finally said okay and took my last four coins, even though they were Russian.

It was a bare room with only a mattress on the floor, an old chest of drawers, two wooden chairs and a small table. But it would do. I got work and left the baby with kindly old Bluma. He cried when I left and she settled him down by talking to him in Yiddish. Soon, he spoke Yiddish better than Russian or Polish. We settled into a comfortable routine; I made enough money for food and rent and to pay Bluma.

Chapter Forty

Dzierzoniow 1946-1950

There was a knock on my door. A man's voice called my name "Sofia, Sofia! It's Michal, Michal, Jacob's good friend. I bring word from him."

I opened the door just a crack and peeked out. In the hall stood a man with stooped shoulders, all skin and bones. His sunken eyes looked at me sadly. I was sure it was Michal. His thin, calloused fingers reached in his pocket and pulled out a piece of crumpled torn paper.

"I promised Jacob I'd deliver this to you when I got free and found you," he said handing me the yellowed paper. My hands trembled when I opened it and smoothed it out.

This is what it said.

My Dearest Sofia,

I do not know how much longer I am to survive this suffering. My legs are like dough, swollen and weak. My teeth are falling out from lack of anything to eat. You are young and beautiful. Take our child and forget about me. Find another who can be with you and who deserves you for I do not expect ever to return to your arms.

Love, Jacob

I read the words but refused to believe them. I invited Michal to come sit down and tell me everything that had happened since he and Jacob left the bakery in Siberia. He told me of chopping wood, mining iron ore and coal, in the most freezing of temperatures with little or no food.

"Poor Jacob was late for work one morning and they beat him and expected him to work until sunset with no food at all. That was the day of the accident when he lost two fingers in the mine. I don't know how he found the strength to keep moving. But he was still alive and there was talk that they might release us all. I was assigned to a coal delivery. I told Jacob that I'd try to escape. That's when he gave me this note. That was the last time I saw him.

When I was almost finished shoveling out the truck I pretended I had fallen and was crushed. The driver of the truck left me, thinking I would die on the spot. After I was sure he was gone, I took off and managed to make my way back to Bialystok and then here. I am so happy to have found you, but I worry each day for Jacob," Michal told me.

I gave half of my food to Michal and he stayed with Bluma for the night. She helped him get a place to stay and work. How she had all these connections, I'll never know. Bluma never left her apartment, and I never saw anyone come or go.

Months passed. I worked the late shift in the clothing factory from one pm to midnight. It was getting colder. I took little Benesh to the convent pre-school as he was quite a handful for old Bluma now. I brought him back before I went to work, then Bluma only had to be with him from about four o'clock until he went to sleep at seven. He was getting stronger, but still had wounds that opened and bled on his side and the back of his knee. I had one little picture of Jacob, which sat on the table and I told Benesh that was his Abba (father).

I had just gotten up and dressed, when there was a knock at the door. I froze. Who would be coming here at that hour? A raspy voice came through the door.

"My Dear Sofia, It's Jacob. I am here if you still want me." Without thinking, I flung the door open. His face was worn and weathered, his once strong body was emaciated and drooping, but I knew it was my Jacob. I threw my arms around this skeleton covered in skin. He reached around me and tears streamed down our faces. I brought him in, wrapped him in a blanket, and fed this poor starving man. With the war and all, we never had a wedding, but we were married just the same, in our hearts.

"What has the cruelty of war done to you, my love?" I asked, not really expecting an answer.

"Doesn't matter now. We survived and we are together again."

Little Benesh woke up, and rubbed his eyes.

"Come and meet your Abba."

Jacob put out his arms. But Benesh ran the other way, saying "boy, boy" ('I'm scared', in Russian). Then he took the picture off the table and said "Abba, Abba" pointing to the man in the picture.

Jacob was still happy to see him, not knowing yet how his little son almost died when the train blew up. I put Jacob to bed and took Benesh to the convent preschool. Jacob was clearly too weak to work, and I had a job so he took care of Benesh most of the day.

Benesh had trouble at school. He told me that when he first started going there, he used to distract the other kids and then steal their butter. When they'd scream, the nuns never knew why. They were all still too young to talk.

The Polish people were really brainwashed before and during the war; they hated Jews. So we worked hard to keep our true identity secret. Only Bluma knew we were Jewish. Some of the Polish people treated Jews as bad as the Nazis did. They thought nothing of spitting in our faces in the street, or attacking us in our homes.

One day Bluma said we had to leave. The landlord knew. We had to get out of the apartment. She had found a four-family house on the edge of town. But we needed money. We gathered everything and went a round-about way to the house Bluma told us about. She had gotten a room in the house across the street from it. I went back and forth with the owner, being very careful to keep our Jewish identity secret. Finally he agreed to take our money and let us rent there. The house had a small fenced yard with two apple trees and a cherry tree. Those were the best cherries in the world, as big as walnuts filled with sweet juicy pulp and such a dark red they were almost black.

I squeezed every coin I earned and we bought goats and pigs.

Benny found a big black stray dog and it stayed with us. We called him Torké, and he became Benny's best friend and protector. Jacob got a bicycle and took Benny all over on it. It was hard to live in constant fear, knowing that any day someone might squeal on us and come to harass, torture, or even kill us.

One day when Benny was in the playground at school, the kids were in line and the boy behind him called him a "Jud, a dirty Jud" and he put a wire around his neck. The nun caught him just as he was beginning to tighten the wire. She kept a close eye on Benny after that. But we did not know how that kid found out. Again, we did not know who we could trust.

So we made plans to get out of Poland. Jacob and I both had cousins in America since before the war, but the gates to the United States were closed. The only refuge for us was Israel. We told Benny that Torké ran away. We sold the two pigs and five goats, which gave us just enough money to go by train to Trieste, Italy and get passage on a ship from there to Israel. It had been a country for only two years but Israel was a place of refuge for displaced Jews like us.

Chapter Forty-One

Brookline, Massachusetts 1990

My baby girl slept and Savta and I talked at the kitchen table as we drank our coffee.

"We had no idea how horrible it was for Jews in Poland even after the war. It's amazing that you escaped all of this. I just don't understand how the Polish people could treat Jews so horribly even after Hitler was dead. They had suffered enough!" My voice betrayed the anger I felt.

"Times were hard. Food was scarce. People needed someone to blame for their bad fortune. Even though the Polish people hated Hitler, they believed the lies he told. The posters, the news... they heard it all, over and over again, until they couldn't help but believe it was the truth. The war ended, but the propaganda they were fed lived on," Savta explained.

"So when you finally got to Israel, life was better, right?" I asked.

"Well not exactly. Now we feared the neighboring Arab countries, and life was hard, but we had hope."

Chapter Forty-Two

Israel 1950-1958

When we arrived in Israel, Jacob was in better health, and little Benny was six. We were assigned to a government-issue tent with seven other couples. No one else had any children. We carried our own water, had to use an outhouse, and the shower was outside. We had rations and looked for work. Everyone here was Jewish, many Sephardic (Moroccan, Turkish, not eastern European or Ashkenazi like us). We didn't have to keep our identity secret and Jacob could use his favorite name, Chaim. Michal came to visit us there. He was so happy to see Chaim alive.

That night we celebrated with a little wine Michal managed to get, I don't know where. Toasting "L'chaim!" (To Life). Benny then chimed in "L'Benesh!" How we all laughed, realizing that Benny knew "chaim" only as his father's name; he had no idea it meant 'life'.

After almost a year, we managed to move to a cabin that we shared with another family in Ness Ziona. We had one room with running water, and a bathroom that we shared with the couple on the other side. There was a little Turkish boy across the road who had no father. His mother beat him and he was always running away. Benny played with him, and that worried me a lot.   Chaim loved ice cream so he made and sold it for a while. One day they came to tell me he had been taken to the hospital with a swollen stomach. It had burst and they had to do surgery. I held his hand and begged him to be strong. He came through the operation and recovered.

He had lost his job at the ice cream factory, so he went back to baking. He worked all the time, day and night. He brought home bread every day, we always had something to eat and we could save money.

They were building new houses in Ness Ziona out of cinderblocks with yards. In a few years, we had enough money to buy one and I was pregnant now. Chaim planted fruit trees and Benny helped with the watering and all the yard work even though he hated gardening; he did it to make us happy. Life was getting better. Benny liked school here and he did well in his studies, but he wouldn't play with the smart kids. He got into fights all the time and ran around with the Sephardic kids who didn't care about their studies.

He learned Hebrew easily and Spanish from his friends. They stole watermelons from a farmer's garden and they played marbles. Benny won all the marbles in the town. I thought "Good, now he'll have to play with his own kind (the Ashkenazi kids)."

#

One day he disappeared. We asked everyone if they had seen him. As the day wore on, there was still no sign of him. Chaim and I worried; as it started to get dark, we were almost convinced that he had been kidnapped by the Arabs. We were going all over calling his name.

Then, from behind a bush, came an answer, "I'll come out if you promise not to spank me."

I knew it was Benny's voice. I was so relieved, and of course I promised not to lay a hand on him that day. Out came this bedraggled little boy with a big smile on his face and a huge sack of marbles. He had gone to the neighboring town, about five kilometers away to play and win more marbles.

"Benny, we were worried sick about you! Why on earth didn't you ask me if you could go before you just took off?"

"'Cause I knew you'd say no."

His father punished him well the next day, and I nagged him over and over about running away from home.

#

Soon our daughter was born. We named her Esther after my mother. What a precious child, looked just like her father; she hated to eat. Finally, we had food and the child had to be forced to eat. Benny was very good with her and would take her in the wagon all over. Three years later, we had another son, fair in complexion and with blue eyes like me. He was quiet and seemed to be studying everything. Benny made him puzzles from pieces of cardboard, and insisted he was a genius. Yes, little Isaac was a very bright child.

Benny grew and was in the Junior Army, a strong and popular boy. Then we got word that some relative of Chaim's was willing to sponsor us to come to the United States, the land of opportunity, where we had heard the streets were paved with gold and everyone had plenty. We couldn't take but a very small amount of money, so we bought gold jewelry, watches and anything we could transport easily.

Benesh wanted to stay in Israel. He kept saying that life was good now and it made no sense to go where they didn't speak Hebrew, or even Spanish. The trees were giving us fruit; we couldn't just up and leave them. Again and again, I told him that "Nothing is forever."

We came to America, to Memphis, Tennessee in 1958 and lived in the projects. When I took Benesh to school, they couldn't understand how he was very good in math, but couldn't read. No one understood that he grew up speaking Russian, Yiddish and Polish, then Hebrew and Spanish, but never had the chance to learn English. They thought he was stupid, so they put him in two English classes. He played football, the only Jewish kid on the team, in the whole school.

All the Jews lived on the other side of town in lovely houses by the synagogue, including our relatives. They acted like they had done us a big favor bringing us here and now we were on our own; no one helped us with anything. Benesh hated wearing long pants instead of shorts and things were not easy.

We all learned English, and heard about a union of Jewish bakers in Boston. So in a year, we went by bus to Massachusetts and lived in a town called Malden. The moving van that had all our furniture and belongings was in a big crash and we never got our stuff. So we started over again. But Chaim had work and Benesh went to high school where there were Jewish, Italian and Irish Catholic kids. Life was finally good. Chaim always said that he was rich, with his four diamonds, what more could he want in life?

PART IV

A HANDFUL OF POLISH SOIL

Chapter Forty-Three

Framingham, Massachusetts 2010

It was a nice spring day and I hadn't seen my neighbor across the street. So I wandered over to pay her a visit, hoping she wasn't sick. At 88, Claudia still loved to cook, but she was physically unable to do a lot. Even though she loved gardening, she didn't get outside much anymore.

As I knocked on her door, I saw a shadow through the lace curtain. When she let me in, there was a worried look on her face, but she perked up when she saw me, and invited me to sit down and join her for a glass of wine.

She took out her special carafe of red wine and I found the crystal wine glasses that my father had given her years ago. Of course, Claudia couldn't serve wine without cheese and crackers. When we were comfortable, I looked at her round face that matched her plump body in a blue silky knit dress. I asked her why she looked so worried.

"Ah, here is a letter from my dear friend, Dorothy, from England," she said as her large, wrinkled hand pulled the envelope from a pile of bills and fliers on the table.

As she handed it to me, she added, "Dorothy says I must write my story before I die, but what do I know about writing? Knitting…now that I can do, but writing? My English friend says my lifetime during the war was an incredible journey, and that's true. No human being should have to go through all I did in those days."

"I'd love to hear your story, and I could write it for you. You'll only have to tell it to me. What do you think if I bring over my laptop computer and type it while you talk? Would that work? You can stop whenever you want to and we'll continue it when I come back again. When it's finished, we can send it to Dorothy," I proposed.

"Oh, would you? Could you?" Claudia asked.

"So, it's a deal! You supply the wine, cheese and the story and I'll get it down for Dorothy and anyone else who wants to read it."

Chapter Forty-Four

Poland 1939

Claudia's story begins…

It all started when the war broke out in 1939. When the Germans hit Poland, a lot of people were running east to get away from them. Many refugees were coming to our town. We read in the papers that Hitler was mad. Then the Russians came at the end of September, everybody said they came peacefully. The Polish army was running from the Germans and now the Russians, they were stuck between two devils. They had no choice.

My family lived near Romania, four miles from the border in the town of Sniatyn. My father was a border guard. My mother, Katerine, sent me to the border to tell my father not to cross over into Romania. The four miles were so packed with soldiers, carriages, civilians, and everyone was crying. They were so confused. Most knew they wouldn't be safe either under Germany or Russia. I was only 17, almost 18. Three guys asked *me* what they should do.

One said, "1 can't leave my wife and children."

The others were resigned to the fact that they couldn't do anything for their families.

The border was full of people and on the other side were piles of guns given up by the Polish soldiers. Just before they got to the Romanian border, I saw a Polish soldier kneel down and gather up a small handful of soil. Then others did the same. They wrapped it in their handkerchiefs before crossing over the border. It made me cry to think that this was their small piece of Polish soil they were taking with them, not knowing if they'd ever be back.

Finally, I found my father.

He said, "tell mother I can't go back, I cannot do anything to help you. I might cause more trouble for you. Take care of the children, you must take care of the children, especially little Raclaw."

He was only one year old. Father made me take an oath not to abandon them and I promised I never would, that I would stay with my brothers Edgar and Raclaw and keep them safe. Since my mother had me do everything for them, dress and feed them and even wash and change their diapers, I knew how to do everything with kids.

The Russian army came to our town. Stalin didn't want to attack Poland. The army on the Russian side was quite good, with Asian Tartars in rags. We Poles kind of welcomed them at first. The criminal element of the town was going to get even. The Ukraines were happy too. Watching the Russian army, they beat up the Poles; they walked and smelled of musk or mink oil used on leather.

I didn't want to go to school and did not know what to do. The kids were told to go back to school. Mother's friend, Mary, had a husband who was also a border guard and his family lived in the guardhouse. The soldiers made them move out, empty the guardhouse. So mother's friend and her three kids came to stay with us. It was crowded with furniture and all our belongings and theirs, but that was okay. We all got along. Mother worked as a nurse and Mary stayed home with the six children. We had all been friends from way back.

Chapter Forty-Five

Trouble in Sniatyn

Then mother got in trouble with the NKVD (Russian secret police, Narodnyy Komissariat Vnutrennikh Del) for helping people get through the border and somebody squealed on her. On February 2nd, the Russian police came with a lot of soldiers and arrested both my mother and Mary late at night. They always came at 12 or 1 in the morning so nobody could see what was going on. There was a lot of crying, my mother made me promise to take care of baby Raclaw and Edgar. The officer said our mothers would be back in the morning.

Morning came and nothing. I was 17 years old and Helen, Mary's daughter and my best friend, was 16. I fixed a little breakfast and went to the jail to see my mother and Mary.

The guy in the office said, "Get out! They are not here."

An officer outside, took the breakfast and asked another guy to take the basket to our mothers. The officer made me sit and he questioned me for five hours; I told him nothing. He kept asking me if I saw Mr. G. and what was he doing in our house. Again and again I told him I didn't see him, I didn't know him. I asked what my mother had done. He said she confessed to it all and he had her signature on the confession in his hand. I asked if I could read what was on the paper that she had signed. The officer wouldn't let me, but he finally let me out. There were a lot of others outside the jail. The ladies were wives of the men who were arrested the same night as my mother and Mary. There were teachers, a retired captain, engineers, professors and many more in the jail. The ladies there talked to me and said they were so sorry. I came back the next day. The officer questioned me again, but he didn't keep me long.

Again and again I said, "I know nothing." (That was what my mother had told me to do if I was ever caught and interrogated by the authorities.)

My mother and Mary had nothing, no clothes, no food; they brought nothing with them when they were arrested. The officers wanted to send the children to the orphanage. Mother had another friend, Padichkova, who was Czech and lived in Poland all her life. She had a hat store, and became our go-between. We could have no one come to visit and we couldn't visit anyone else, we were completely alone. Padichkova talked to somebody and she got advice that she passed on to me. I had to say I was 18, and the authorities left us alone for a while.

The convent was dissolved and three nuns lived in the same building as us. The NKVD started 'visiting' us in the middle of the night, militiamen and Russian soldiers. There were a lot of rumors about transports leaving for Siberia. Almost all the stores were robbed; even the shelves were taken. Jewish merchants owned most of them. Padichkova told us that a reliable source informed her of another train leaving on the 13th of April, next Wednesday.

Chapter Forty-Six

Leaving Home

One night we heard a knock, different from the others. It was very hard, loud, impatient, and scary.

"What are we going to do?" I asked Helen.

The electricity was cut off, so we had no light or radio.

I shouted through the door, "Please there is nothing here, we have no guns or anything."

Then I opened the door. Ten or eleven Russian soldiers and militia barged right in. The head officer had them search the house. They found nothing. One of the policemen kept staring at me, a rather handsome fellow who almost looked more German than Russian, but when he turned his head, there was this ugly red mark on his temple. The NKVD officer opened his briefcase, and pulled out a paper.

He said, "By order of the Russian law, we are to transport you to another province."

I screamed and screamed! The bad guys were stunned.

Then the officer shook me and said, "Stop screaming or you will go as you are now."

I stopped my hysterical outburst. Helen and the officer told me to pack. Edgar dressed himself and Raclaw. I could feel myself getting angrier. Those soldiers were stealing everything! I asked the Russian officer to have them open their pockets, and they emptied them of lots of our things. I packed pots, pans, basins, dishes, food, camera, and everything the soldiers took out of their pockets. The Russian officer would not let me go to the attic for the food we had stored there, because I needed to get the ladder and they did not trust me.

Soon we were loaded with our stuff in a wagon. From where I sat, I saw the nuns peek around the curtain; they blessed the children, looking very sad. A little later, sitting in the wagon I started to laugh. Yes, I was laughing. Helen thought I had really lost it.

As we went through the center of the town, there was not a living soul, only the sound of the wheels and the horses. I hoped someone would come out and be a knight in shining armor; someone big and brave to stop them from taking us to the station. But he didn't show up.

Chapter Forty-Seven

Framingham, Massachusetts 2010

"Oh Dear! How could people have been so ruthless? Six children…and you weren't even Jewish," I almost shouted, unable to contain my anger.

"That didn't really matter, as long as you or someone in your family didn't do what the government wanted, you were the enemy." Claudia tried to explain.

"Even so, it's like people forget they are human," I added.

"I think there is some gang mentality, like the worst kind of peer pressure. There was one soldier who seemed different from the rest. He didn't rummage through our stuff, just kept an eye on us, and he almost had a sad look on his face, until he realized I was watching him. Quickly he turned as if to be sure to hide the awful red mark on the side of his forehead. He never spoke a word, and made me feel as if he too was thinking of hiding. He was very strange. After all these years I can still see his face in my mind."

"I suppose there was a lot of brainwashing to make those soldiers feel like they were doing the right thing, for the future of their country, almost a warped kind of patriotism. Maybe it is true that all is fair in love and war, or at least in war?" I asked, trying to make sense of it all and to quell my anger at the total lack of compassion shown by the soldiers.

Claudia reached across the table and took my hand. Here she was comforting me, and she was the one who had gone through all this. She stood up, took the wine decanter, and poured us each a second glass of red wine.

Instinctively I picked up my glass and we toasted "To survival!"

"To kind neighbors and caring people everywhere!"

A few days later I got home from work early and headed to Claudia's house, anxious to hear more of her story.

Chapter Forty-Eight

Pig Base 1940

We got to the train and got on board; each cattle car had so many people, and then the sliding doors were slammed. The windows were all covered with boards and it was stifling. Women were crowded; they screamed and made noise. Some boards were removed so at least there was a little light. Still, you could only see through a crack down low. There were two big shelves one on top of the other for sleeping and a little hole in the floor for a 'toilet'. Travel to Siberia took three weeks on this crowded train. There was no chance to wash or change clothes. All we were given was a pail of water for drinking and some bread for 46 people in the cattle car. Raclaw was always crying and got an awful diarrhea. You can't imagine the foul smell of pee and poop and unwashed bodies.

#

We got to Pig Base in Kazakhstan. There was an animal slaughterhouse and 'barracks' made for animals, no floor, just sand and boards and one big door. We gathered whatever boards we could to put on the floor to sleep on. We stayed there about a month. They took everyone of working age to dig peat (sod) from seven in the morning to seven at night. This was cut into bricks and dried for fuel.

After that they took us to board another train to Siberia. When we finally got off, we were at a tannery where they processed animal skins. We had one room in a barracks made of logs for the six of us. We slept like sardines, if one person woke up and turned, everybody else did too. The worst part was the bed bugs, pluska. We tried to get rid of them by putting hemp that they make rope out of, around the bed. But the smell of raw hemp was too much, worse than the bed bugs.

We were starving. I was selling all the things we brought with us on the black market, which was blooming. There was no food in the store. Russian women would test the flour by spitting on a little in their hand. If it wasn't smooth, they knew it had been mixed with ashes or some other stuff. The Russians called us Bourgeois. They liked to have our things.

I wonder, to this day, what kind of a man the NKVD officer really was. What did he think about sending six children to that awful place? He had no choice as an officer, but what did he think as a person?

Chapter Forty-Nine

Sick Brothers 1941

The life there was very, very bad. Raclaw got sick with measles and I had to take him to the hospital and he was not quite two years old. He was screaming when the nurse took him and they wouldn't let me go to the room with him. They made him put on a hospital gown and I took his clothes. The next day I came to see him; they laughed at me and wouldn't let me in. The next day I came again, still they wouldn't let me see Raclaw. For six days in a row I showed up at the hospital, and still they wouldn't let me see him.

They sneered, "you are stupid," and made fun of me.

They said that mothers don't even come and you are just a sister. There were rumors that they poisoned the patients and I was so afraid that they would do something to him. I came every day, in spite of what they said. On the tenth day I told them I was sitting on the stairs until they would let me in to see him. They laughed and laughed. Finally one nurse took pity on me and she told me to watch the first floor window. I was so happy to see him. You just cannot imagine. He saw me too and then he screamed. I was so glad that he was strong enough to cry. The next day, they said I could bring his clothes and take him out of there.

When they brought him to me, he wouldn't let go of me long enough to get him dressed. The nurses all gathered around and watched. They thought this was a great show. Finally one came over to help me and the two of us got him dressed. He still wouldn't let go; he clung to me so tight. I remember this clearly, even after all these years. It was too far to walk carrying him, about three miles, so I got into the 'bus'. This was really a truck with boards in the back. Raclaw, such a little kid, held me so tight...he couldn't let go. Finally when we got back to his brother and the others, he relaxed. I understood what he was going through. He had no food, no family, no home, no holidays. He only had me.

#

The next thing that happened in Siberia was awful. My brother Edgar, who had been a sick child in Poland got pneumonia. The winter of 1941 was so harsh, he was very sick and coughing all the time. We were in a small room with one little window covered with ice an inch thick and the walls had frost like in the refrigerator. We slept all together with no heat in the room. I was messaging him and trying to give him compresses on his chest. There were no medicines, drugstores or anything. He was coughing and coughing. I was working at night…sewing sheep coats for the army.

At work, the woman sitting across from me asked, "What's wrong, Claudia?"

"I can't take him to the hospital, I heard they poison sick

people." I answered.

The lady told me there was a Russian doctor there. She told me his name and where to find him. As soon as I got back to our little room, I asked Helen to put a fresh cover on the bed for Edgar and I was about to leave to go get the doctor when Edgar had a hemorrhage. Blood was everywhere. They cleaned as best they could. I went to the doctor's place, banged on his door and begged him to come help. He insisted that he wasn't a doctor. I got on my knees and begged and cried. His wife finally told him to please go. He reluctantly agreed but said we could not go together.

"You go first, then I'll follow," he told me.

It was about two miles; I didn't trust that he was following me. I thought this was his trick to get rid of me. But shortly after I got back to our room, he did come. I let him in and he examined my brother. I was embarrassed because we couldn't clean up all the blood, even though we did the best we could, so I told the doctor the blood just came. He said that was actually good, to help get rid of the disease. The doctor said he needed a warm climate and good food. I was exchanging everything I had with the Kazaks for milk and butter. Edgar never gained weight, but he survived the winter.

#

Then came summer and the Red Cross. I went to the consul to get some food, and they had a Polish doctor there who opened an orphanage in that town. I thought I'd put my brothers there so they would at least get food. I had nothing else to barter. The kids were there and I'd get to see them every week. The poor children you should have seen them; they were skinny with boils all over their bodies, lice in their hair, and tattered clothes. There were these two little Polish girls who never spoke a word of their own language.

Chapter Fifty

Leaving Siberia 1941

The Polish president was exiled and he worked with Churchill. It was the end of 1941. Stalin released the Polish prisoners so they could go and fight Hitler. When they first got out, they were a sorry sight. They wanted their families to be let out. First the men went and they joined the army, then the refugees and the Polish government took care of the orphans and any Polish children kept by the Russians.

In February, I heard the orphanage was going to move out of Siberia. I asked to leave Siberia with my brothers. I was told that I couldn't, that I was too old. I thought, *if I keep them here we all die; if I let them go, I'll never know what will become of them.*

A Polish woman asked me why I was crying. I told her I promised my mother and my father I would take care of them. She took me by the hand and we marched right back. She really let them have it at the consul.

She was shouting at them "these little kids have no mother, no father, no food, no place to call home. This is all they have, a sister. You can't separate them now, after all they have been through."

On and on she ranted. Finally the consul wrote up an order to let me be a nursemaid. Then pretty soon the transport (cattle car) came. We got into the car: two teachers, about 20 kids, an officer and me traveling south. We came to Samarkand.

The officer said, "I need two people to go to the Red Cross diplomatic station".

When we got out of the car, we saw the station in the cold, misty, dripping rain. Then we saw several farmers' carts filled with bodies like logs….many refugees had caught typhoid fever, they were so weak and had died. The officer wouldn't risk us going through the streets, so we got back in the transport and traveled on.

Chapter Fifty-One

Ashkhabad 1941

We came to Ashkhabad on the border between Persia and Russia. About 200 children were there before us, waiting to go to Persia. We were late…20 odd kids and a few more who were very sick. There we had good food, not too bad. Someone got mumps and had to be quarantined. We were supposed to leave for the Persian town of Mashhad. Then a Polish woman, Steffa, a nurse at the embassy, knew we were going in the morning and she wanted one last chance to have a little party with us. She invited Helen, her aunt and me. The guard wouldn't let us go in. Steffa had a key and we went in the back gate. We had a good supper; we talked and laughed. About 11 we left, going to the embassy through the back gate…it was surrounded by the NKVD. A mouse couldn't get away. We couldn't be on the street. We *had* to go through the front door.

We saw the guardian tied up in a chair, they were questioning him, "Who are you?"

I was so scared! The NKVD guard looked at us. I was afraid, so I took advantage of the commotion and sneaked out, then darted thru the veranda to my room to get to my brothers. The Russian soldiers came after me, one pounded on my door. I refused to leave the room. He could not go in there, and I refused to come out. My room was on the side entrance and I watched out the window. A big black limousine pulled in. The doctor, ambassador, attaché and the whole staff got into the big limo. They all had diplomatic passports and they just disappeared. Then the teachers, and the others wondered what to do. We thought we'd never get out of there now. No soldiers came to pick us up, no one.

One day passed, then two. A platoon delivering Red Cross supplies came. There was a truck of Polish soldiers and we wanted to leave with them. One of the soldiers had a Russian girlfriend, and he wasn't sleeping in his room. He sneaked around and told the NKVD that he had orders to take the children, and they agreed to let us go on the third day. We never saw any of the embassy people come back. While we didn't see the NKVD, we didn't expect to. They didn't do any business during the day; they worked at night so nobody could know what they did or talk about how bad they were.

The little boys were all collecting bottles and glasses in Ashkhabad.

When I asked, "What do you need the bottles for?" the kids wouldn't tell.

We packed what little we had into the truck and went to the border. They kept us there for about three or four hours in the hot sun, checking everything.

They asked why the boys had bottles and I told them "I don't know" because I didn't.

The kids told them "Water! Water!"

At last the officers let us go and the barrier was let up. After they were sure we were in Persia, all hell broke loose. I tell you, it was fantastic!

Shouting "Long Live Poland," the boys threw all their bottles back at Russia. The Persian soldiers took the kids, bought them candy and everyone was happy.

Chapter Fifty-Two

From Mashhad to India

There were 200 kids waiting for us in Mashhad. We stayed there another few days, Dr. Kanarsky was there and he took us all and he examined each child to be sure they would be able to make the trip. He said I couldn't go, because I had an irregular heartbeat. Again, I had to beg and plead to stay with my brothers, after all we had been through, I wasn't about to leave them now! So he let me come. Dr. Kanarsky was so wonderful! He took care of all the children. To this day, I don't know how he did it, I thought he would have a heart attack before our journey was over. He couldn't sleep, watched over the sick kids and put them into his station wagon. We traveled in many jeeps through the hot, dry, dusty desert. There were two boys who were special, and Dr. Kanarsky put them in my care.

The trip took three days, I think. When we approached the Afghanistan border, the Persians sent us a military convoy to guard us. It was very dangerous because Afghan bandits attacked transports. So when we stopped to sleep, the jeeps were all in a circle like a wagon train. Dr.Kanarsky gave strict orders not to leave. I don't think he slept a wink.

We came to Zahedan (in Persia), the last town before India. What a beautiful place with colorful, patterned carpets throughout. We had baths and slept on those carpets, unbelievable. It was like an inn. We were in the big building, in a huge hall, over 2000 kids and then the grown-ups too, who were taking care of the kids. We stayed there and then the doctor said that there was to be no contact with the people while we were in that city. He was afraid that the men might kidnap a girl. They were men, and there the women were covered and here were girls, nice looking for them to see. We slept there one night; then we had to go when the train came.

We were traveling one day or maybe two, I don't know for sure how long we were in the train. Suddenly it stopped, could not go any longer, we were at the town of Quetta (it's Pakistan now). It was a beautiful place where we stayed for more than a month, with English people. The English soldiers were stationed there at the compound, their barracks. The English women used to come and dress up kids; they used to take us to a restaurant, the meals were fantastic; we had showers, bathrooms, everything, and all the good facilities. The kids made a show for the English people and they danced the Krakowiak, the Polish dance from Zakopane. The women hurriedly made costumes and they were flabbergasted! They loved it. Then it came time for us to go. They gave us a big send-off.

They packed the train and went to Islamabad where the Polish Embassy executive from Istanbul met us. There were some changes, not everybody could go where we were going. We were on our way to Balachadi, and that's where there was a rotten priest, Pluta. He had over 500 kids there. Some of the orphans had rich relatives and the Embassy was to pull them out. The two special boys and Kanarsky left the transport. (Many years later I heard that they were Jewish orphans and had managed to escape to Palestine, now Israel.)

Chapter Fifty-Three

Balachadi in Karachi, India 1942

So we came to Balachadi and recruit training started. That idiot Pluta took the kids; they were starved in Russia. He was very cruel to them. They had to march in a straight line, sing every morning and pray when the flag was flying before they could go to the living room and the dining room. One time when there was rain, you know, the monsoon season, the kids tried to hurry up and they broke the line. The whole barracks of those kids didn't get breakfast.

I was in bad with him, because he opened my letters and was looking at who I was corresponding with, and I got a letter from an English boy. He wrote me in French so not everyone could read his letters. He was a good-looking one too! I met him when we were passing from Persia to India. I saw the open letter, and I went right to the priest's office. I knocked and opened the door. The priest was having a ball with his lady. I walked right in on him. That was trouble for me.

I asked, "Why did you open my letter?"

"This letter has been opened by the censor, there was nothing for you to see."

You couldn't write a letter from that camp or receive a letter that Pluta didn't read. If he didn't like what you wrote, he wouldn't send it. So we had to put up with him. That was terrible. While we were in the camp I was 20 years old. He made me work in the hospital giving medications. I mean, I'm not a nurse, but I worked there. There was a Hindu doctor and a Polish doctor. The Polish doctor was very nice and she liked me. When the wife of the Polish ambassador came to the camp to pick up all the girls to send them to the convent to learn English, she told me to sign up for it. I told her I couldn't leave my brothers.

She said, "and how can you take care of your brothers when you don't know English and you have to work?"

So I signed up. I had a good friend who promised me she'd look after my brothers when I went. (She's in Canada now.)

So, I was in the hospital and the doctor came and said, "I'm sorry you scratched your name off the list."

I replied, "No, I didn't cross off my name."

Now you know Pluta did! But the kind doctor put my name right back on it.

The priest was mistreating kids; he was beating them. This one little boy left the camp; he wanted to go to the ocean. We lived right on the ocean, and there was really nothing else there, just the desert, and Maharaja's palace on the edge of it. Pluta was coming back from town, he caught the boy, beat the hell out of him. The little boy was on crutches. The Indian doctor was crying. Why would he do that? Pluta had sticks and belts to punish the kids and he used them.

Chapter Fifty-Four

Framingham, Massachusetts 2010

So Claudia and I had finished another part of the story.

"I am really confused. How could Pluta be a priest and be such a bad person? If he mistreated the children, he didn't have a heart. They let him be a priest?" I asked.

"My friend," Claudia replied, "how can you be so naive? In every profession, there are good and bad people. Priests are no different. Think about all the child abuser priests in our time right here in Boston!"

"So what makes them evil instead of good Christians like they are supposed to be?" I asked.

"Who knows? Something in their minds just makes them think they are better than everyone else and so they have a right to prove their will and power over others with cruelty and punishment."

"I guess. But you would think that priests would be better than the Nazis...humankind is strange."

"Ah, we'll never have all the answers. So what do you say, how about a refill on the wine? Do you like this hot habanero cheese?

Polish people think spices are dill, salt and pepper. But in India, they know spicy like the Mexicans."

I laughed and got myself a glass of water to drink with my cheese and crackers. Claudia laughed too.

Kazio, her husband, came in from the garden with two bags full of tomatoes.

"Here, you must take some home. Pick nice ones and fill a bag," he said as he put the crumpled plastic in my hand.

"Thank you; nothing tastes as good as a fresh red tomato still warm from the sun."

As I filled the bag, Claudia smiled.

"You know, after going through hard times, we know how rich we are. It is our pleasure to share the wealth."

It was a few more days before I found time to get back to Claudia's for a visit. When I did, the story returned to India.

Chapter Fifty-Five

The English Family

I went out of Pluta's camp to stay in the convent. I got sick. While they were treating me for malaria in that hospital I got infected with smallpox. So I was rushed into isolation with two women taking care of me, the nurse and her helper, the Untouchable. After a month, when it was hot I got hot and red in the face, when it was cold, I was blue. But I didn't have the pox on my face because they were treating me very well with special oil, and they tied my hands so I didn't scratch. No water, no bath, only some lotion, they changed my bed two to three times a day. The first water I got was from the tree that the oil was from. They boiled the leaves so it was dark green; oh it felt so good. When I was better I went back to the convent.

From there I got an invitation from the English family to be the companion to Mrs. Pearl. She had four children, three boys and a girl named Dorothy. Teresa was another girl they picked. I didn't know what to do. But they said this was an invitation I had to take. Teresa didn't know much English. I knew a little more, which I learned at the convent in Karachi. We traveled from Karachi almost to Kashmir by train. It was too hot to stay in Karachi so we went to the mountains. How did we get there? I don't know. We saw the Taj Mahal. The lady told me in a letter, when you go to Agra, that's where the Taj Mahal is, stop by and see it. So when we got there, we took a tonga, that's a two wheel, horse-drawn carriage, with the driver sitting in the front and one seat in the back. With just two wheels you know you are kind of going to flop, you're afraid you are going to fall out of it. But oh, it was beautiful... so many people, you had to take off your shoes. The guy there had to be given something; all he had was paper money. *I'm not going to give him paper money,* I thought, so I put in some change.

Then we went back. The stationmaster put us in a second-class coach with 'air conditioning'. In the middle of the room was a big block of ice that was too cold. In India, it was impossible. You had to baksheesh, baksheesh, baksheesh, give them money. We finally got there.

When we came the ladies picked us up. Teresa was with her sister and I was with Mrs. Pearl. Then we went further on to Nainitol and Saranaga. There we could see Mt. Everest. Saranaga has a big lake with houseboats and we lived on one for a month because it was too early to go up the mountains. No car drove there. You went by horse. They told us not to walk because of the low air pressure, thin air. So if we went anywhere, we had to call for a horse. At first I didn't know how to ride it. I thought you just sat there and said 'Go'. But I had to learn to go with the horse, like I lifted myself up from the saddle. You know, if you just sit, you'll bounce up and down, and owww. I had the experiences ...unbelievable. We stayed there close to a year.

Now India was getting ready for independence. I knew what was going on. I corresponded with my brothers and my girlfriend. Mrs. Pearl told me to come with them. They wanted to take me to England. I was like family. I didn't do anything.

She had five servants and told me, "don't spoil my servants."

So I kept an eye on the youngest son. But the servants made my bed, they drew my bath, they did everything. What a life! I was meeting all all high class guests. They had a dinner party for all these people. They were very nice, especially the father, Mr. Taleko. He was a regular guy. One night we were sitting at the dinner table, one guy brought his girlfriend. They were going to England pretty soon. The British command in Delhi was going to dissolve, and they were talking about what they were going to do in England. My boss said that he was going to open a butcher shop.

The other guy, was a snob, and said, "How could you?"

"What's that? Why not?" my boss replied.

Then they looked toward me.

I said, "Oh, I have to go take care of my brothers. I have been away from them two years and that is enough."

I said good-bye. That was about 1945-46, the time of repatriation.

Chapter Fifty-Six

Kelapur 1946

I went to the camp in Kelapur. My brothers were still in Balachadi in Karachi and Pluta would not send them to me even though my father wrote to him and asked him to. In Kelapur, the refugee camp was near Bihar. That's where the orphanage was, with about 5,000 children. I went in there. I came to the BaliBada, as the camp was called. I was taken to Mrs. Badich. She was a finance executive for the camp. The people in the camp were getting money each month for their food; they cooked their own food. She was the person who gave them the money. The interpreter, Mahavshi Helen was from high society in Poland and she spoke French. Anyway, I came in and Mrs. Badich was talking and I was answering her, answering in English. Helen looked at me.

Slap! Helen slammed her open hand on the desk and shouted, "give her a job! I'm tired of serving the Polish Commandant, the English Commandant and you. I need help!"

So I was going to be her help. Right away I got the job with Colonel Neat, the British Commandant, because we were under British rule. He was an old guy, when he walked I thought his knees would collapse on him. He told me all about himself and the time he spent as the British attaché in Moscow. I told him about where I was and my mother was still there.

"Oh, I have a friend in the British Embassy in Moscow," he told me.

I don't know how the letter got through the diplomatic mail, but in about five weeks, the Colonel came and told me that the letter got there and his friend said he could start, but it would only worsen her situation. If the British were asking for her, then they would think that she must be important. My mother was considered a spy. That was why the Russians put her in jail; that's why he said they better not get involved. She would be a lot worse off than she was.

Then Colonel Neat had to retire. He was corresponding with a blue-blooded Russian from the court, the Czar's; she was in Yugoslavia or somewhere, I don't know. She was bugging him or something.

He kept asking me, "Do you think I should marry her?"

I said, "I can't tell you that." (I was 22.)

I don't know how old he was, but he had false teeth and he was always clicking them. He was bringing his clothes to the office to be fixed. I had to take them to the shop, where the girls were learning to sew.

When they saw me they would scowl and say, "Oh, here she is again!"

They hated that I brought them these old, old clothes. They

told me to collect the money and get him new shorts and throw this stuff away. But, that's the way he was. He didn't marry the Russian lady. He left, and I didn't know where.

Chapter Fifty-Seven

India's Independence 1947

India got freedom from England and India could not afford to maintain the camp. So the UN and all the other repatriation agencies came to the camp and they were sending counselors to Poland. Australia wouldn't take any; New Zealand took some. America wouldn't take any. Most of the rest of them went to England and some back to Poland. My father got back to Poland and my mother got back from Russia to my grandmother's place. That was where we had all agreed to meet some six long years ago.

My father said, "come back."

I said, "no, I'm not going to the Russian country any more." (I knew too many things from being with all the high class people and important government officials.)

Father wanted me to send the children. I didn't know what to do. Edgar knew his father and mother because he was ten when we were separated, and now he was about 16. But I had to send Raclaw, too, even though he was too young to remember his parents. To this day, he cannot forgive me. He used to take me for his mother.

"Mommy this, Mommy that," he always said.

"I already told you, Raclaw, I'm not your mother; I'm your sister," I told him over and over again.

When I sent Raclaw home with Edgar, my mother still didn't understand. She was stupid; she didn't ask the doctor to explain.

Raclaw used to say, "Please may I have this, thank you," but no name when he talked to my mother. He was always running away. To this day he is angry with me. I couldn't do anything or I would have broken my parents hearts.

My mother asked me, "How did you raise this kid?"

She blamed me for Raclaw's behavior with her. She just didn't know what we went through, and how I tried to get him to understand that he was really her child.

Now you ask, "How did I get to England?"

Chapter Fifty-Eight

To England 1947

You wouldn't believe it. In the camp, there were about ten or twelve older officers, who were too old to do anything, so they were sent to the camp. But, they couldn't pay them any more. Well, the army went back to England, so these old officers couldn't get any money. They wrote to the military office in Poland, to please take them back.

When the letter came saying, "The Polish people will send for you in due time."

I translated for the Indian Commandant, I said it read "You are called to the army now."

Then I told the old officers, "I'm putting my life on the line for you guys. Now you need to send a call for me to join the army."

They went to Egypt, and there they went to the office, and the office sent me an application so that I could get from India to Egypt. The English paid for it.

Before I left, the Commandant got the letter.

"How the hell did you send them back to Egypt? They didn't know anything in the office in that country!"

"See how much a little translator can do? Of course I couldn't tell the Commandant. I played stupid," Claudia chuckled.

When I got to Egypt, they didn't want to take me. What they were going to do, I didn't know, but I had documents. There was only a small business open, a few tents with remnants of people. They gave me the uniform and they said I should help them in the office with stuff, with what they were doing. I got a tent with a nice Jewish girl and she was in the Polish army and was going to Palestine; she was engaged to a Polish officer too. I just wondered if they would accept her and what they would say about him. Well, it was touchy. The army was decreasing now; everyone was leaving. They thought I was Jewish because there was another fellow, an older man also waiting to go to Palestine. He came to me and talked in Hebrew or Yiddish. I didn't understand.

He said, "What? You are not Jewish."

When the army in India folded, I took a ship. Who found me on the ship? Mr. Teleko, he was going to England. He invited me to dinner there, first class. We talked. It was unbelievable, to find him on the same ship now, and to think I used to be with his family, his wife and all their children. He was very nice. Mr. Taleko was with a young man on the ship. He thought I might fall for the young fellow. We ended up in Liverpool.

I had the damnedest luck, getting off the ship, we had to present documents, you know, all our paperwork. I gave mine to the guy, the Polish officer.

"You can't get in," he told me. "These are not good papers; you are not army. You cannot enter."

"So where am I supposed to go?"

There was some other English guy who took me. They put me in a waiting place, where women were changing from uniforms to civilian clothes. I stayed with them in that place and was able to call my brother Henry, who was in England after serving in the army during the war. He came over and stayed at that camp with me.

Henry thought he could take me to Dorothy's to figure things out. He had a heart like a barrel, like a cracker barrel...so big. I stayed with him in that little camp. They gave me a job in the library there with civilians and everyone else.

Then things were straightened out and I contacted Kazio from Sniatyn. We had grown up in the same town in Poland and corresponded through all of this. Kazio came over to where Henry was and rescued me. He was in England all this time. We had wanted to keep in touch, to know what was happening to each other and to our families. Kazio became my husband.

Chapter Fifty-Nine

England to America 1948-1951

A few years later, I wrote to Colonel Neat when I was in
England. I tried to get hold of him because and he had given me his
address. He wrote to me. Colonel Neat even invited me to the high
officer's club in London. It was after I had my babies and no decent
clothes, I wasn't from England. When I went, he introduced me to
Polish aristocracy. I felt so small; he even introduced me to the Duke
and Duchess.

Mrs. Badich also went to see me in England. I didn't know
how she knew where to find me, but she did. She came over to our
small house in Riceslip in Middlesex and I was feeding my baby son.
This was 1949 or 1950.

In 1950, Kazio's brother and his parents went to America. So
we followed, and first lived in Cambridge, Massachusetts. Then we
managed, just barely, to be able to buy a house with three bedrooms
and no basement in a new neighborhood in Framingham. This was
1957. Now our two children have grown up, married, and have had
their share of sorrows and hard times, even in America. In 2006, our
daughter died of lung cancer... oh, how we tried to get her to stop

smoking. But Kazio and I go on. He is 94 and still gardens, vacuums, takes care of our dog, mows his own yard, and shovels the snow in New England, as he has done for many years.

Chapter Sixty

Framingham, Massachusetts 2011

We sat Claudia's kitchen table, just thinking of all it could tell if it could talk. Our wine glasses were full and the cheese and crackers were waiting to tangle with our taste buds.

"Well, Claudia, I am so grateful to know your story. If you give me Dorothy's address, I will be sure to send it to her. Do you ever wonder why you survived?"

"It's hard to believe all of it and how horrible some things were. But there were also those kind and incredible people like Dr. Kanarsky, Padichkova, my nurse, the Untouchable and so many more. Kazio survived, only a very, very few of the RAF (Royal Air Force) bomber pilots made it out. He was shot down and was held prisoner for a time. But that's about all I know. He always thought that once you got out of the bad times, you left them behind and got on with your life. He is one of those people who took all the horrible memories and put them in a chamadanchick, locked it up, and never opened it again."

"A chamadanchick?"

"You, know a small suitcase, here you might just call it

baggage."

"So, is it a good thing, or a bad thing to try to lock it up and leave it all behind?"

"Hmm…I don't know. I just couldn't forget. All the nightmares and the burden of being responsible for my brothers were too hard to get out of my head. The worst part was that my mother never forgave me for making Raclaw call me mother, which of course I did not. But she never listened to my side of the story. Raclaw never forgave me for not coming back to Poland. What did he understand? But Edgar knew and to this day is such a good friend as well as a brother."

"You know my mother-in-law felt that these stories needed to be told. Too many people in my generation don't care; they have never known war first-hand. Those who have suffered understand, those who have listened, know that horrors are possible. Those who don't care won't be willing to stand up for what's right." I said.

"I know what you mean, the way politics are going in this country, both parties are being ruled by the rich. The economy is in a state of inflation; pretty soon even a loaf of bread will barely be affordable. The dollar is not backed by precious metals anymore. So it will become worthless, the economy will go down the drain. This is exactly why Hitler was able to make promises and get people to believe that things would be better under his rule. What's to keep that from happening here?" Claudia posed a very good question.

"I don't know, but it's scary. Everyone I know assumes that

the economy will continue just as it is, and as long as they don't lose their jobs, it doesn't affect them. Boy, I sure hope you and I are wrong."

"But come what may, today we have what really matters, good friends, good neighbors, and our families. Your children are something for you to be proud of; both have college degrees and are good human beings. You can't ask for much more."

"Let's toast to good friends, good neighbors and family! Claudia, you know you and Kazio are part of our family too!"

PART V

THE STRANGER ON THE PLANE

Chapter Sixty-One

Flying out of Boston 2013

Tears were about to spill out of his deep blue eyes. Dark circles underneath them made me think he hadn't slept in days. His bowed head and sagging shoulders were reminiscent of a sad, lost puppy dog. He lifted his hand and pushed his fingers through his tousled blond hair. As people piled up behind me waiting for me to claim my seat, I hesitated to disturb this man in the brown jacket and pressed trousers. But he was in the aisle seat and I had to get past.

"Excuse me." I said motioning to my seat.

He didn't even look up, seemingly engrossed in his own thoughts.

"Excuse me." I repeated a bit louder.

Again, no response; I lightly nudged his shoulder. His head popped up as his straight hair flew.

"Entschuldigen sie mir, bitte?" (Excuse me, please?)

"Ich gehe dort." (I am going there.) I replied in my almost forgotten, broken German as I pointed to my seat.

"Ya," he said quietly as he stepped out into the aisle to let me pass.

"Sprechen sie etwas English?" I asked.

"Aber naturlich. (Of course) Sie sprechen Deutch auch, nicht wahr?"

"Nur ein Bisschen; Ich habe so viel vergessen." (Only a little, I have forgotten much.)

"So, you going to Germany?" he asked.

"Finally I am on my way to Europe. Ever since high school, I've wanted to go to Poland, Germany, and France. Now I'm finishing my 'bucket list', traveling to Nowa Ruda, Poland where my father was born in 1923. I have only a tattered picture of an apartment building with an x over the window of the room where he was born. I'm in search of my father's past, so I'm starting there. Then I'll go on to Germany, trying to trace his journey to Hamburg. What about you?" I explained.

"Strange, I came to America in search of my father's past. I'm going back home to München."

"So you were in Boston?" I asked.

"Yes, I went in search of my uncle."

"Did you find him?"

"Yes… and no…with the internet nowadays you can easily find a person physically and I met him for the first time in my life. But no, I still know nothing about him or my father."

"But if you met him, surely he talked to you."

"Only on the surface. He told me things like his years as a

professor at MIT, and his home and family in Cambridge. But he refused to discuss anything even remotely related to why I came. He thought it enough to offer his condolences on the death of my mother."

"I am so sorry to hear you have lost her. Are you all alone in the world? Is that why you went in search of your uncle? What did you want to know from him?"

I couldn't help but blurt out all the questions flowing through my mind.

"My uncle's childhood, how he got to America, anything and everything he knew about my father. But you know, some people refuse to deal with the past. It's as if they buy a new suitcase to start a journey, and tuck away all of their memories in the old one, never to open it again."

"Yes, I know what you mean. My father rarely opened his suitcase, and only for a few quick glances, but luckily my grandmother told us about the 'Old Country'. Was there no one for you to talk to?"

"Only my mother, but her life before I was born was locked in a trunk. She told me that my father died from the war. I have no siblings and when I got old enough to do the arithmetic, dying in the war never rang true. I was born in 1947, after the war ended. The more I questioned her, the tighter her lips became. She would only say that it's a mother's duty to protect her child."

"Do you have a family of your own?" I asked.

"I do have a wife, but we could never have children. Maybe that is for the better," he replied as he turned his wedding band on his left hand.

"Here we are talking about our lives and I don't even know your name. I'm Kenda, married with two grown children on a fact-finding mission. Next time my husband will come to Poland to find his family's roots."

"My name is Felix, but I am still searching for who I am. So many questions with no answers." His voice drifted off and he went back to a deep, pensive stare.

After a long silence, my curiosity would not be still.

"What kinds of questions are you trying to answer?" I asked.

"Oh, you wouldn't be interested, deep philosophical ones, that probably have no answers anyway."

"Like what? Try me," I said defiantly.

He was not going to treat me like some bimbo. I had experienced a lot of life in 65 years and read and studied enough for two PhDs.

"I wouldn't want to expose you to all my issues. You should enjoy your flight."

"Listen, I've spent a lot of years in chemistry research labs, and then decided that I really enjoyed working with people, so I went back to get my certification as a clinical psychologist and I love this. So I'm sure your questions and issues would be more interesting to me than any reading I could do on this trip," I said in an attempt to get him to open his chamadanchick.

"Okay, let's start with: where does evil come from? I mean, if a person is a criminal, do they pass their evil on to their children, like genes?"

"I never really thought of it that way. I would say, of course not!"

"So how does a person become evil? Is it something that's taught?" He looked straight at me with piercing blue eyes that demanded an answer.

Oh, dear! now what have I started! What should I say? Just think about the question.

"I… don't really know. But I'd surmise that it's what they are exposed to, like violent video games in this day and age, having parents who don't care about others, even their own kids, who are quick to blame anyone but themselves for all their troubles. Maybe people get a little bit of power and begin to think they are much better than everyone else. It's like delusions of grandeur, but always at the expense of others. Like the plantation owners and the slaves in our American history."

I continued talking about the Stanford prison experiment in the early 1970's where a psychology professor set up a simulation of a prison in the basement of the building. Using student volunteers he randomly divided them into prisoners and guards for a planned 14-day experiment. It took just a few days for the prisoners to become demoralized, depressed and helpless. The guards wasted no time treating their prisoners as less than human; quickly they became sadistic and lost all compassion for their prisoners. It became so horrific that the experiment had to be terminated in just six days.

About one-third of the guards were leaders in the despicable treatment of the 'inmates'. Even when other guards attempted to object or do small favors for the prisoners, the sadistic leaders used peer pressure. It clearly showed how easily people can be disconnected from humanity by setting up conditions of power for an elite group.

"So what you're saying is that it's not 'nature, but nurture', the environment and the circumstances and not the genetic make-up of the person that makes him evil," Felix restated.

"Pretty much, but there's more to it. What becomes acceptable behavior in a culture or situation shapes a lot of it, like the media and political assertions nowadays spread the propaganda of extremists. When people hear something enough times, at first, they really don't know what to believe. Then they fall hook, line and sinker for the propaganda, believing it's the truth…the only truth. Just talk to a die-hard Republican who is convinced that all the Democrats have ruined our economy with their give-away programs or the die-hard Democrat who will convince you that we must take care of everyone around the world, even if we can't afford it. Politicians are quick to criticize, but seldom propose solutions that are carefully studied and can be implemented effectively. They rely on propaganda to get elected.

Everything in America has been made so complicated that it is rare to find anyone who knows and understands the facts. For example, the legislation that has become 'Obamacare' is over 2,000 pages. The health care system is so bogged down in management costs, insurance claims, contractors, advertising and other middlemen that the money left for taking care of the patients is a small fraction of what it should be. But no one knows what it really is. Yet propaganda has everyone believing that socialized medicine is a bad thing, or that Obamacare is no good. No one can really tell you what they mean by socialized medicine or what Obamacare actually does or doesn't do."

"I think I understand what you are saying. Things that have both elements of good and bad can be labeled one or the other. Evil can become the norm, even considered good, because it's disguised as something else and both the perpetrators and the victims are brainwashed by propaganda, nicht wahr?

So let's move on to the next dilemma. If a person is descended from a criminal or an evil person, should he feel guilty? Should the plantation owner's kids feel guilty for the injustices done to the slaves?"

"Of course not. The kids had nothing to do with it. The plantation owners and their farmhands treated the slaves as subhuman, not the children. In some cases the children even befriended the slave's kids. It's natural to be kind and to reach out to others. We should all listen to the child in us more often. Unfortunately, the kids became victims as well, being punished for associating with those who were 'beneath' them.

In order for the whole system to survive, the cotton plantations and southern economy, slavery was essential. So whites had to be taught from an early age that the slaves were inferior and deserved to be worked hard like animals and be punished if they did not or could not. As subhuman, they didn't need nice things, 'book-learning', or anything more than a shack to live in. They were the property of the plantation owner, and as such, families could be separated. I think this chapter in our history is shameful. It's horrible what was done, the entire industry of slave trade. But as an American today, born many years after all this occurred, I am in no way responsible and cannot personally feel guilty about it."

"Mmm-hmm. I hear what you say…and I like the analogy." Felix hesitated as he spoke, furrowing his brow.

"Analogy to what?"

"Ach, nichts, Nothing," Felix shifted uneasily in his seat and he stared straight ahead.

Had I said something wrong? Wait! Where was that conversation going? Oh, maybe we were both just tired since we needed to be at Logan Airport at the crack of dawn. That was just his way of politely trying to make me shut up and leave him to his own thoughts.

After an announcement from the pilot, I leaned my seat back, relaxed, and closed my eyes.

Chapter Sixty-Two

Pondering the Idea of Evil

When I woke up, I looked around and my sleepy brain retrieved the thread of the conversation with my seatmate, Felix. It was about evil, hatred, prejudice and bigotry.

As I pondered these qualities, I thought that they were born of greed, of an insatiable appetite for power; then they were spread like a virus by propaganda. There was no inherited component to it. Evil grew out of disconnection, which allowed people to see themselves as better than others. The plantation owners saw themselves as separate from the slaves. Their skin color was an easy way to be disconnected from them.

It felt so odd to have a philosophical conversation like this with a total stranger. I thought about more recent news. Random acts of evil: school shootings, Danvers teacher murdered, Sudbury student stabbed to death... I tried to make sense of it. Connection came from compassion; where there was none, there was isolation, desolation. This was the landscape where the seeds of evil sprouted and violence, fed by frustration, exploded in the mind of the perpetrator. It became contagious through media exposure, a kind of propaganda. A worthless life was given an opportunity for fame.

What did it take to kill someone, an individual or an army? Dad became a marine, to fight for the United States, to become an American citizen. He said that recruits were disciplined, torn down to nothing and turned into fighting machines. When they went out on the battlefield they saw only 'the enemy' and 'us'. He was sent to the Pacific theater and had nightmares about the "Japs" for many years after the World War II was over. Kennedy referred to it as "demonizing our adversaries and thinking war is inevitable."

Woodrow Wilson spoke about "making the world safe for democracy." What did this mean? What about those who didn't believe in democracy? If we didn't understand them, then we undermined them because of their beliefs. When someone was different from us and we couldn't relate to them, they became the enemy. It was only a small step to hating them, demonizing them and trying to destroy them.

Take the marathon bombers. One had said that he didn't have a single American friend, even though he'd spent years in this country. How could he have understood what we believed, what we Americans thought of as democracy and freedom if he'd never had a conversation about it with a friend here? Instead, a little brainwashing on his trips to his homeland must have made it easy for him to demonize Americans. Once he'd done that, killing them became his duty. He was only trying to rid the world of evil, or was he?

Chapter Sixty-Three

Felix's Story

Felix was clenching a brown leather folder filled with yellowed, crumpled papers. He slammed it shut when he saw me catch a glimpse of it. The date in one corner was 1930 and it was in German script, but that was about all I could make out.

"So, Felix, did you rest at all?" I asked.

"Ach, Nein!"

"You know, I'm a trained psychologist, and it is almost always helpful to talk. If you'd like to tell me more, you'll never see me again after this trip and I'll respect patient confidentiality. It could help you come to terms with the loss of your mother and the mystery of your father," I said in my quiet, convincing voice.

"Ya, maybe, what have I got to lose?" he said putting his seat back as if pretending it was a shrink's couch.

"So where do I start?" he asked.

"Anywhere you want."

"When I grew up with just my mother and me in our apartment, she claimed that she never lied to me. Mother told me 'Your father died from the war,' and nothing more. For many years, I was haunted by that statement. Father's picture sat on a shelf. Even that bothered me; it showed only the left side of his face. The same for their wedding pictures, his face is turned toward Mama, instead of the camera. Mama told me he had an older brother, Wehrner, who was sickly but really smart, especially in math."

"So that's the uncle you saw in Boston?"

"Yes, a physics professor, in his 90s, but his brain is still sharp. He thought I took the easy way out, studying the humanities instead of science. As a kid, I had few friends, most had siblings and fathers, so I was always the shy, odd kid. Books were my refuge, especially social studies, that's why I'm a history professor at LMU in Munich, that's Ludwig-Maximilians-Universität. History and music kept me alive. Mama loved classical music, especially Mozart, and growing up it always seemed to be playing in the background."

"So all this sounds pretty normal. And, of course, you'd be pretty devastated when your mother died, since she was the only close, stable person in your life growing up, right?"

"Well, it wasn't just her death. That was bad enough, but the hidden secrets for all those years," Felix replied.

He continued in a whisper, "My mother said 'Your father died from the war.' I always thought it was the same thing as 'Your father died *in* the war.' Mother never really lied to me."

Chapter Sixty-Four

The Secrets in the Trunk

Felix continued, "The trunk at the foot of mother's bed was always locked. Many times over the years I looked for the key, but never found it. After she died, I finally broke open the lock."

"So what did you find in it?"

"Some beautiful embroidered linens that had been folded for so many years they just fell apart at the creases, an old uniform, some pictures and this 'diary' of sorts."

"What kind of uniform? What's in the diary?" I asked, anxious to satisfy my curiosoity.

"It was an SS uniform, brown shirt, swastika armband, even the black boots, still shiny, and an earth-grey jacket with an eagle badge. Ya…he, my father, was a Nazi. I think that's what Mama meant when she said it was a mother's duty to protect her child."

Now all the questions he asked about evil made sense. I should have figured this out.

"So does the diary give you any more clues?" I asked.

"Ya, it looks like he wrote bits and pieces and probably tucked the pages into his boots, and only put them in this brown leather folder after the war."

"Are you willing to share some of them with me? You'll never see me again after we get off this plane."

Felix grasped the folder tightly and looked me straight in the eye.

"Opening these 'secrets' just might help you to understand and deal with the past better. I am a 'shrink' you know," I told Felix as I patted his arm trying to reassure him.

Chapter Sixty-Five

The Beginning of the Diary

Felix hesitated, then opened the brown leather folder, and translated the words as he read them.

I am so excited, so privileged to be a leader in the Hitler Youth! Finally I can do something better than Wehrner, besides sing and play the violin. All the boys think music is for sissies. It's my chance to prove myself, to bring honor to Germany. I will make a good soldier and prove I'm a man. Who needs all that math stuff? Hitler will make our Vaterland great again, and I'll be right there making it happen. The only thing I wonder is what will become of Max? I always thought he was a nice kid and like me, his big brother was perfect, so we got along. Now, he's a dirty Jew, his family got rich off us. Maybe I should have had more sense about him sooner. Well, my new life will be parades and training sessions, school without Juden, and maybe soon a promotion to a be one of the 'Führer's men.'

The Next page is dated 1931.

I am one of the loyal favorites. At only 15, they are making me a Junior Schutzstaffel (SS), complete with uniform, black breeches, boots and brown shirt with an armband! I learn quickly everything they teach me; I was always good at memorizing music and lyrics. My parents named me Wolfgang Amadeus, thinking I'd spend my life as a musician. Hah! Not me! I'm the best at keeping the beat and can march for hours on end. I lead Hitlerjugend Parades. The SS officers who manage our Group recognized this and promoted me. My first assignment was to track down the truants. No matter how much we publicize events, some children are still missing. I did not march in this parade; I had more important work to do. With three other officers, I went to the houses of the missing kids and got them to the parade where they should have been!

It was Saturday and we started as soon as the parade began. At the first house we banged on the door and just as our leader was about to shove his way in, an old stooped fellow came and opened the door. He told us there were no children there and he was too weak to get to the parade himself. Our leader acted like he didn't believe him and made him walk to the basement stairs. Then he took the butt of his rifle and smacked the old guy on the jaw. The old man stumbled and fell down the stairs.

"That'll teach him, and any kids hiding in that house will

know we mean business!" our leader announced.

I kept a straight face even though I was appalled at the cruelty. That man did nothing; maybe there were no children there.

Our officer said, "And that gentlemen is how it's done!"

The next house was empty, much to my relief. We broke in and searched every corner, under the beds, in the basement and in the attic.

In the next house, there were supposed to be two boys, the father was gone, we barely waited for the Frau to open the door. I tried to act like I was mean and angry, shouting in the Frau's face. She told us the boys were very ill, and we went to their beds. The older one was pale in the face. Something didn't seem right, but I felt the head of the little one. It was hot. I moved away from him so I didn't catch whatever he might have been sick with. Then I lectured the Frau, and pretended that I was the meanest one of the bunch.

"The older boy is ten, nicht wahr? He should be in the Jungvolk and marching in the parade." I shouted at her.

She told me "next year he'd be ten, and yes, he'd join and be in all the activities." Then I saluted "HEIL HITLER!" and headed down the stairs. Our leader nodded his approval at me. But I was left thinking those boys didn't act like sick kids with fevers, especially the older one. If he was burning with fever, his face should have been red and not pale. Little sick boys whine; they don't lie there in bed with their arms at their sides as if petrified. I hoped the Frau heeded my warning, I'd hate to see anything bad done to them.

When Felix finished the page, I gasped, remembering my grandmother's story.

"Are you okay?" Felix asked. "You look like you just saw a ghost. Are you sure you want me to read on?"

Chapter Sixty-Six

How Can they Hate Him?

"Yes, definitely, you must read on."

"Are you sure?" Felix asked.

"Yes," I answered firmly.

Felix turned the rumpled pages. Some were torn and water-stained. He held one up, tilted it on an angle, and tried to read it.

" *...moving up the ranks. .....excited about the honor of accompanying Hitler to cities for speaking engagements... great and powerful leader... Mannheim town hall...brilliant speech from the balcony...*

Ach! Such a horrible act! Who would do such a thing?...

Of course, Hitler was pushed. He could have died! ...Landed in the bushes...I was the first to get to him and help him to his feet. As soon as he was standing I saluted him, and rushed him over to his waiting car as he shouted that no one will embarrass him, without paying a price. I never could have imagined a man so angry!

How is it that even the best leaders have enemies?

"Ach, this is so hard to read, looks like it's been folded and stomped on, let's just go on to the next paper here," Felix said as he pulled out another page, and continued reading.

Back at headquarters, I was summoned to the office to meet with Bruno Gesche and Walter Schellenberg. Gesche is a scary guy, who'd beat you up in a minute if he even suspected that you were not loyal. He greeted me with his arms crossed over his chest, standing very tall.

"So this is the youngster who kept me from killing those Hitler haters in Mannheim?" his deep voice chilled me to the core.

Schellenberg replied with a plan he'd hatched. Saying I was loyal and only needed more experience; he had an important and dangerous mission for me. I needed to get into the spy network. The Luftwaffe made a successful raid on Coventry. Surely Churchill will retaliate. My job is to intercept their plans and to see to it that the city the RAF (the British Royal Air Force) attacks is Mannheim! I am given careful instructions that I must memorize and carry out. One misstep and I am dead. If the bombing doesn't happen as planned, Gesche will find me and take care of me himself. Now I know this is not the life I want, but it's too late. How I miss school and music and my family. Instead, I live in constant fear, an isolated soul not knowing what tomorrow holds.

Chapter Sixty-Seven

The Undercover Mission

Felix and I were anxious to turn the page. His hand shook, and I thought I knew that all must have turned out okay, because we had many more pages in this diary of sorts.

My life is a nightmare, running from place to place, not knowing who I can trust, all alone. I don't dare put any of it on paper. If I am caught, if I make just one mistake, I am dead. With anything written, all my contacts will be dead too.

Finally, I think my part of this year-long mission is accomplished. I sit in the office as the code is sent. Now it's up to fate. Will the British believe it? Will they follow our wishes? Lives are held in the balance...my own as well. It feels as if human life really doesn't matter that much anymore.

Everything is for the cause, for the Vaterland.

And if Schellenberg's plan succeeds, where will I be sent from here?

Chapter Sixty-Eight

A New Assignment

"So what happened? After Mannheim got bombed?" I asked.

"How did you know Mannheim got bombed? We didn't read anything about that yet," Felix said, furrowing his brow.

"I do know a little history," I replied quickly not wanting to talk about the hours I had spent in Heidi's kitchen.

"There are three or four pages of unreadable, worn writings that I can't begin to make sense of. But this one is okay," Felix said as he began reading.

Now I am to be part of the Judenrein in Latvia, plans to rid the country of those despicable Jews. They sure do make a lot of work for us. I have been assigned to Einsatzgruppe A under Paul Degenhart. The ghetto in Riga is just being established and it will soon be filled. The ghetto will not be so bad for them; plans are for us to find a suitable place for trenches to march those pigs to, where we'll be able to shoot them and have them fall into their own massive grave. I am part of the group scouting out the location for all of this to

happen. Riga is too swampy, not good for disposal of lots of
corpses. We need elevated ground on the north side of the
Daugava River, within walking distance of the ghetto.

So the six of us set out in the area of the Rumbala
Forest. I left the highway and the rest of the group and followed
a path of tall pine trees. It was quiet and peaceful, such an
irony when I thought of what it would be in the months to come.

Then I noticed a girl in the distance, carrying a large
cloth bag. When she heard me, she began to run. That made
me determined to catch her and find out what she was doing
there, thinking I could have some fun with her if she was a Jew
and then leave her dead…one less to deal with later. I caught
her easily, grabbed her by the arm, and looked into her
eyes…blue ones… filled with tears and fright. I was stunned as
her humanness touched my heart. I let her go. She ran on
through the woods. Then I looked around me to be sure no one
saw this; it could have meant a severe reprimand or at least
much teasing by my fellow Nazis for not taking advantage of a
good situation. It was okay though, with those blue eyes, she
couldn't have been a Jew. But I know I will wonder for the rest
of my days where she was going and why…

Felix kept reading, but I was lost in my thoughts. *God gave
Savta blue eyes for a reason. Her mother was right that she was their
only hope.*

Chapter Sixty-Nine

The Music Lady

Felix continued reading...

On the train to Czechoslovakia, I was wondering what they would have me do next. Der Führer was expanding his Jew-hunt to this part of Europe. I thought I'd be rounding them up at night for Theresienstadt. Prague had a reputation as a great cultural city, with many Jews as part of its aristocracy. There were no special places for us, so the SS had already taken over apartments in this affluent city.

As I sat on the deep red brocade chair, I felt like royalty. Mother should have seen me. Light sparkled in symmetrical designs on the long, deep cherry wood dining table. The patterns flickered and drew my eyes to the dusty crystal chandelier above.

I wondered who lived here, what kind of people they were, and what they did to gain these riches. I had to stop my mind from going down that path, as I knew where they had gone, either dead or barely alive in Theresienstadt. That was one of the better camps; it was the model we showed off to the international Red Cross three times a year.

I hadn't seen my own family in years. It's 1943, I said good-by to my parents and Wehrner more than ten years ago. I had no idea then that I might never see them again. What are they doing? Are they still at home? Papa is probably a soldier fighting for the Vaterland, Wehrner too. Is Mama all alone?

The last few days and nights have been taxing. I have been forced to work at the camp in the mornings, separating the Jews collected at night, tearing families apart, even taking children away from their mothers, that was the hardest at first. But you just couldn't think about it. I kept telling myself that this was important work for the Führer, these were not real people but ugly Juden. Another officer seemed to have his eye on me all the time, just waiting for me to slip up. When I was finally dismissed, I returned to my apartment. No one knew that I was there alone. The other soldiers had found themselves women to spend their off-duty time with.

Piano music drifted up from the floor below, soothing my soul. It made my existence bearable. The melodies made sleep possible.

When I awoke and put on my uniform, the music was still there. Maybe I was going mad, just imagining it. After all, for nearly ten years, I had been doing this work that tears my mind in two. Der Führer and Der Vaterland above all, but what has happened to our cities and the people, many who were not Jews? I questioned all the destruction and that confused my feeble brain even more. I wondered if Wehrner had any answers to this dilemma; he was always the smart one; I wondered where he was, what he was doing.

I had better not be late. As I hurried down the stairs, the music got louder and I glimpsed a Mezuzah on the doorframe with the name Sommer. The music faded as I ran down the stairs, but I tried to keep it in my head.

The dreadful days of deportations stretched on. But my apartment was my refuge where the music continued for hours at a time. Until one day, the music stopped and there were voices, the sounds of furniture being dragged across the floor. I had to find out what was happening. The Mezuzah was missing from the door. All of the neighbors were grabbing the lady's things and a small boy about 5 or 6 years old clung to her skirt. Word had come that she was one of the next to go.

After the commotion settled, I slipped into what was left of her apartment. I told her that I hoped she'd return, that I admired her and her playing for hours, and that I'd miss the patience and beauty of her music more than she would ever know. I thanked her for continuing in spite of the times.

She tilted her head to the side and mumbled something about how we are all good and bad, and today I was the only human of all the people in and out of her apartment. Everyone else was coming for whatever they could get.

Was that irony? I was the Nazi, the horrible bad guy. Or was I?

Chapter Seventy

A Wolf in Sheep's Clothes

About six tattered pages later, I finally brought my attention back to Felix's words.

….such a dangerous situation…the NKVD has already taken over this part of Poland, they marched right through Romania. I was separated from the other SS officers. I was left behind, too far to make it to the truck. If the Russian Police caught me, I would have been dead for sure.

I slipped into the alcove by the doors to a building. It was deserted and locked. They were parading up and down the streets in this border town. Luckily I was thin and my uniform was the color of the shadows. There was nothing there, a few scraps of paper, a few leaves and a piece of wire, which I picked up. A dog barked at a trash barrel across the street. A soldier marched closer to my hiding place; he was about my size. I grabbed the wire just as he passed by me. With both hands I swung the loop of wire over his head and around his neck, pulled it with all my might and dragged him into the alcove. I reached in my pocket and stuffed my handkerchief into his mouth, then pulled as hard as I could on the wire to be certain he was dead. I had never changed clothes so fast in my entire life. Smoothing out his uniform, I peeked around. All the other soldiers were occupied with the dog and whatever was in the trashcan.

I went down the street in the opposite direction. That quick change made me part of the NKVD, a Russian soldier. Good thing I learned some Russian and studied how this army behaved as part of my training. It was strange, being the enemy.

I fell in easily with the other Russian soldiers who were raiding houses in the night, and sending the "unwanted" to Siberia. Twice we went to this apartment with all children, five or six of them. The two oldest were in their teens. This night our head officer, Leonid, decided we were going back there to get rid of them for once and for all. First we banged on the door, then barged in and searched the place. The oldest, a pretty Polish girl turned out to be feisty. As we searched, she kept insisting that there was nothing there. But this night was different than in the past. Leonid had a paper with orders to transport them to Siberia. He read it. The pretty one screamed her head off! We were all shocked and didn't know how to react. Leonid finally grabbed her and shook her, telling her to stop, get dressed, and pack up, which she did.

We all started helping ourselves to anything we wanted in the house. The feisty one was angry, almost cute, and she yelled at Leonid. Imagine that! Here she is being taken away to Siberia and she shouts at Leonid that we are stealing their things and he must make us empty our pockets.

Even more amazing, Leonid listened to her! He ordered us to empty our pockets and we did. Then she packed all sorts of stuff including all of our loot. We finally got that motley bunch of kids into the horse-drawn wagon to take them to the station.

It was nice working at night like this because the streets were empty and there were no lights, except maybe a small candle in in a window, where I glimpsed a nun peeking through the curtains.

Where are the parents of these kids? The Papa is probably in the Polish army. But, the mother, she must have done something wrong, in prison? They weren't Jews, but they needed to be deported as no one could support a whole apartment full of orphans, during a war. When I thought of that brave and spunky girl, I couldn't help but admire her grit. I'd bet she would survive this war.

Chapter Seventy-One

The Last Page

The pilot announced that we needed to prepare for landing.

"Felix, can we skip to the end?" I asked.

"Ya, but it is the end," he replied as he turned to last page, the one that was unwrinkled.

1947

Our little child will be born soon. You must forgive me, Dear Gisele. You must understand, it's not that I don't love you and our infant. It's just that I do not deserve to see the child grow up, after all those I denied their families.

You know I cannot sleep at night. My mind is totally overcome with guilt, with nightmares and horrors that I helped to perpetrate. I became a monster when I joined the regime. I cannot deny that I had a hand in destroying the lives of many, many innocent people. I will make such an unfit father; I cannot hold down a job. I am no good for you any longer. You will be strong and you will protect our child.

Someday our child will find my brother, Wehrner, and maybe find understanding. I cannot expect you to know my anguish, only to forgive it if you can and to carry on with your lives.

With this I will destroy the ugly mark on my temple. In just a few minutes the bullet will penetrate it and end this monstrous life.

POSTSCRIPT

Heroines of the Kitchen Table is a work of fiction, but the Grandma, the shoemaker's daughter, the mother-in-law and the Polish neighbor all existed. Their names have been changed but many of the dates and places are factual, based on research, passports and other artifacts, which I inherited. The Reisepass on the book cover is a photo of Grandma's passport from 1936.

My deepest gratitude goes to the four heroic women who were willing to open their trunks and their hearts to me. They shared their stories, their kindness and their laughter with me through the years. I had only to listen. It was such a privilege to write their memories in hopes that they will influence others in some small way. I wish I had asked more questions of them. For example, how did Grandma actually get from the forest to Mannheim and Hamburg? In this and other parts of the novel I exercised my own creative license.

Many current events, stories, books and movies influenced this work as well. The Holocaust Memorial Museum in Washington helped to set the stage for many scenes and characters. Movies and books that had a significant impact on my thinking and writing included: "The Boy in the Striped Pajamas", "Night", "Sarah's Key",

"The Zookeeper's Wife", "The Book Thief" and many others.

Perhaps, most important is the documentary "Hitler's Children" about the surviving children of Hitler's henchmen. It is from this work that the character of Felix was created, including the philosophical argument about the inheritance of evil, which came from one of Goering's descendants. The brother and sister were voluntarily sterilized to "cut the line", believing that being descended from evil people made you evil also. Felix, his father, and his uncle are fictitious characters created to try to explain in my own mind how these inhuman actions could have been carried out.

It was the news story of the Czech pianist, Alice Herz-Sommer the oldest holocaust survivor, who died recently at the age of 110 that inspired the name and the musical aspect of the character of Felix's father, Wolfgang.

It is my sincere hope that this novel will make people realize that there is good and evil in all of us and that kindness and compassion are the most important values. These are what make us human. Further, the idea that history repeats itself is often true because seeking power at the expense of others causes polarization and extremism. In order for extremist ideas to flourish propaganda is used. It justifies disconnecting and demonizing those who are different based on religion, ethnicity or other qualities. Most people don't realize that everyone suffers. The power-hungry who put themselves above others can bring only destruction to *everyone* in the end.

Our best defense is education. We must teach our children critical thinking, to evaluate information and be aware of the power of propaganda. We must teach them compassion, to understand and relate to others as human beings. It is up to us to make the world a better place and to treat others as we would like to be treated, no matter what the circumstances.

ACKNOWLEDGEMENTS

Special people have made this work possible. In addition to the four heroines, who are all deceased, my husband, Ben, gave me inspiration, time and space to complete this novel. My children, Lisa and David, believed in this project and in me. Lisa's photo (of the silhouettes) adorns the cover. Thank you so much for your incredible support.

My sister, Jane Holzapfel, proofreader and fact-checker, added some memories, and provided invaluable encouragement for my work. My brother-in-law, Elliot Lach, confirmed the merit of this novel and added some valuable pieces of Sofia's story.

My writer friends gave me many good suggestions and editorial comments and pushed me to move forward to the end. These include: Matt Osber, Linda de Cougny, and Jennifer Graham. I would be remiss if I did not thank Carrie Johnson who gave me the confidence and courage to "re-invent" myself as an author, without regard to my age.

Dear friends, Paula Fillion, Baiba Ozols, Jeanne Fagone, and Holly Smith heard bits and pieces of the story and validated the need for this to be published. Thank you to Bev Machtinger for sharing her parents' stories from Lodz to Dachau, and the horrible treatment by the Polish people that continued after the war. This emphasized the importance of understanding that propaganda lives beyond conflict.

Thanks to Rachel Martinez and Nina Deuschle, my patient listeners, who helped me transform these tales from my past into legends for the next generation. I am grateful to Sandra Petrakis for sharing her words and deep emotions from her recent trip to Dachau. This helped make the airplane discussion with Felix seem real. Many thanks to Nicole Savoie, the best editor anywhere, whose candid comments, great listener's perspective, and attention to detail were invaluable.

I am grateful to many more friends who added their stories and words of encouragement. Thank you all for the part you have played in helping to bring my Heroines to life again.

ABOUT THE AUTHOR

Carol Lynn Luck (aka. Carol Lach) was the high school English student who hated to write, as she felt she had nothing to say. Her PhD in the sciences taught her to think critically and she published many articles in scientific and educational journals in the 50 years after high school. Upon retiring, she realized how rich and varied her "nine lives" had been in scientific research, teaching, marketing, technology, parenting, management, entrepreneurship, education and most important, being a friend.

This, her first novel to be published, grew out of listening to the stories of others. She has much more to write about, and has a second novel, *Gym Class Klutz*, nearly ready for publication.

Carol lives in Framingham, Massachusetts with her husband. She is passionate about providing a meaningful, quality education for all American children. Carol's hobbies include doing math puzzles, reading historical fiction, cooking, enjoying others' kids, writing about education and visiting friends. She blogs at **www.daythechalkboardfell.wordpress.com** and her email is CarolLynnLuck@gmail.com .

Made in the USA
Middletown, DE
31 March 2015